Way Off Base:
A Brother's Best Friend Romance
Book 3 in the North Bay Series

By Stephanie Giese

ISBN-13: 9781737206873

Cover design by: Rachel Adams-Howard
Interior illustrations by: Abigail Giese, Eddie Giese

Published by Binkies and Briefcases, LLC

Printed in the United States of America

Dedication

*To everyone putting themselves last and taking care of everyone else,
I see you. I'm glad you found a moment for yourself, and I'm honored this
is the book you've chosen to read with that time. Grab a cozy blanket and
a cup of something warm. They might only be fictional, but while we're
together here in North Bay, I promise to deliver all the happily ever afters
you deserve.*

Content Warning

Way Off Base contains adult content and is intended for readers over the age of eighteen. The reader should be aware that the following pages contain adult language and on-page consensual sexual encounters. This book features discussions and depictions of prescription medication, a family member's history of addiction, parental abandonment, and the physical, mental, and sexual health of the main characters. While I hope Jordan and Shelley's story helps you feel seen, the content of this book is not intended to be a substitute for professional advice. Although research was conducted for the health conversations in this book, all evidence and medical advice contained within is anecdotal and fictitious. It is always recommended you consult a licensed physician or mental health practitioner for your real-life needs.

A Note from the Author

Thank you for visiting North Bay! The books in this series are standalone romances with interconnected characters. You do not need to read the previous books in the North Bay series to be able to enjoy this one. However, there will be some references and callbacks that are spoilers if the books are read out of order. For that reason, I do recommend readers start with Book One, *Out of Left Field*, which will give you the best understanding of this town and the quirky characters who live here.

Way Off Base is Jordan and Shelley's story. This is Book Three in the North Bay series. It takes place in the same time frame as Book Two, *Right as Rain*, so you will notice some overlapping events. This is a fun, lighthearted brother's best friend romance, but there are also serious themes in this book which may be triggering to some readers. I strongly recommend checking out the content warnings.

Each book in this series depicts mental health treatment in some capacity. This time I also wanted to tell a story about women's health and the struggles we can face seeking treatment. So often, stories centered around women's health focus solely on pregnancy. This is not that kind of story. Shelley is a strong, smart woman prioritizing her own physical, mental, and sexual health.

Jordan's journey to discover his own sexuality in the context of a loving straight-passing relationship is a story I wanted to explore because it mirrors my own, and I have not seen a story like his represented elsewhere.

I also feel the need to say Shelley and Jordan's experiences with neurodiversity and sexual identity are uniquely their own. While I hope you relate to the universal themes in this book, this story is not intended to be a reflection of anyone else's lived experience, except perhaps my own. This is an Own Voices book.

Playlists for each book in this series are available on Spotify. You can see the *Way Off Base* playlist here:

Chapter 1

Shelley

The thin layer of paper beneath me crinkles as I shift on the bench, trying in vain to make sure both of my bare cheeks are covered by the flimsy half-robe the doctor's office provided. I flip through a boring gynecology magazine I took from the display on the wall, thinking about how I'd rather be just about anywhere else on the planet. When I stumble upon a familiar name, I suck in a short breath. Josephine Wilson and I were on the high school track team together for years back in Idaho. I've seen her talking about her work on social media, but I had no idea my old friend's research was getting this much attention.

The headline reads *Primary Parents Don't Put Out: An Equal Workload Achieves Higher Success Rates, In and Out of the Bedroom*. It's a well-cited and nuanced discussion, examining the silent effects of female domestic labor on relationships, which is exactly what I would expect from Jo. She's out here with a doctoral thesis helping thousands of couples navigate the orgasm gap in their long-term partnerships. Meanwhile, I wouldn't even qualify for her studies, because I've never been in a relationship longer than three weeks.

I snap a photo of the article and text it to my sisters. Madison responds right away.

Mads: *Whoa, that's cool! We know a real-life scientist.*

There's a knock on the door, and I put the phone down as my new doctor enters with a nurse following behind.

"Ready to get started?" Dr. Dupree asks.

I nod as if anyone can ever be fully ready to be held open with metal tongs and probed under fluorescent lights. Should I have waxed for this? I swear, sometimes taking care of my health feels like submitting to some kind of perverse alien abduction.

"I understand we're here today because you reported some changes in your arousal and sexual satisfaction during your annual exam," she says.

"Yep. That about sums it up."

Her probing only takes a few minutes. Then Dr. Dupree peels off her gloves and tosses them into the trash can. "Everything looks fine here. I'd say it's good news, but this also means I don't have any definitive answers for you yet." She rolls her stool a few feet backward, over to her laptop, where she types something in my chart.

I lower my feet from the stirrups and sit up, wincing at the gobs of lube squishing between my legs. "That's good, I guess."

Except it means I'm no closer to understanding why my body is a traitor, and now I probably need to schedule even more appointments if I want to solve the mystery of my own vagina and why she hates me.

Just call me Nancy Drew. I should be in my Family Law class right now, but instead I've spent the morning spread eagle over a paper sheet on a cold table, and I'll have to present my professor with a doctor's note just because I want to be able to rub one out like a normal person. Unfortunately, the Magic O is still elusive for me.

I wish this weren't a big deal and I could just shrug and move on with my life, but I'm too young to be drier than the flaking skin on the bottom of my great-aunt Mildred's feet. My body doesn't respond the way it should, which makes me feel broken, and it makes dating impossible. It's hard to connect with other people when I'm in my head the whole time I'm being touched.

"You don't appear to have any physical abnormalities, but I see there's a stimulant listed here, along with your birth control. Sometimes these medications do have sexual side effects, unfortunately, as I'm sure your prescribing physician has discussed with you. No matter the cause, what I can do now is offer you an estrogen cream to increase arousal and pleasure. I think there's a good chance it may help."

"Okay. A cream sounds easy enough. Is it expensive?"

"Usually under twenty dollars for the cream, depending on your insurance. And I'd like to run more bloodwork to give us the best picture of what might be going on. I believe that will be fully covered. We can do it here before you leave."

I cringe. I hate needles. "And if this medicine doesn't work?"

"Let's cross that bridge when we come to it. Right now, I'm hopeful it will be the boost you need. You could also consider a change in your other medication if you think it might be helpful."

I blink at her. If *I* think it might be helpful? She's the doctor here. What do I know?

"I've seen a shot come up in my searches, but I never gave it serious consideration," I tell her. See: fear of needles. "And honestly, I never thought to bring up my sex life with my psychiatrist." Going off my ADHD meds is not an option. Law school is intense, and the level of competition is high. I won't be able to get through the rest of the semester if I can't focus. If I exercise a little more and eat healthy foods, my body should be able to do this stuff on its own, right?

Except, obviously, it isn't. So...

"Can you tell me more about the shot some people get in their G-spot. Do you think I'd be a good candidate?" I gulp.

"That would likely be a question for a plastic surgeon or a med spa. The shot you're referring to is more of an augmentation and not something we offer at our practice. It's an injection of hyaluronic acid. It claims to last up to four months, but I haven't seen any studies on long-term use. Is that something you think you might pursue?"

Do I want to find yet another doctor so I can pay them to inject acid straight into my G-spot on the off-chance I might be able to feel something down there? I don't know. Needles? Vagina? Big yikes. I clench my thighs at the thought. I've seen how much pain my mom is in after her IUD insertions, and it sounds like this might even be worse.

Dr. Dupree adds, "I do have to warn you, the shot is generally considered an elective procedure, so I don't believe it would be covered by insurance."

"How much does it cost?"

"My best guess? Between one and two thousand dollars," she says in her professional, matter-of-fact tone.

I swallow again and try to keep my face neutral. I'm glad women have options available, but two *thousand* dollars? And I'd have to do it three times a year. Not just needles, then. Expensive needles.

Bet the insurance companies have no problem covering boner pills, though, do they?

Is it worth spending two thousand dollars every few months for a chance to be able to come?

My first instinct is *Hell no! I don't want a shot there, and I'm definitely not willing to pay six thousand dollars a year for the privilege*. Dr. Dupree doesn't seem super keen on the idea either, since it's not something she offers to her patients, but I guess I should consider all my options. Although, I think the cost alone just made the decision for me. That's more debt I would have to pile on top of what I already owe. It's not like I can call my parents and ask them for money for this. Then again, are fear and money good enough reasons to give up a chance at healing my body?

"I'll need to think about it." I sigh.

"You do that. In the meantime, I'll write the script for the cream. Can I do anything else for you today?"

Dr. Dupree has a reputation as the best gynecologist in the D.C. metro area, that's why I was referred here, and even she can't pin down exactly *why* my body can't achieve orgasm.

Behold, my befuddling beaver, folks.

"Why are these decisions so hard?" I groan. This whole situation feels hopeless.

"I can also refer you to a therapist or another psychiatrist," Dr. Dupree offers. "Sometimes the issue is up here." She taps lightly on her temple with one finger.

"Thanks. I already have one of each." I'm out here collecting doctors like Pokémon cards on my quest for sexual satisfaction. Obviously, it's not going well.

She says she'll also call in a new script for my birth control pills to the pharmacy. Then Dr. Dupree leaves, and the nurse stays to draw my blood. I can't watch, but thankfully, she finds my vein with no trouble and it's over quickly. The nurse nods and says a quick goodbye before leaving me alone to get dressed.

I hastily use a wad of cheap one-ply tissues from the box on the counter to clean myself up before digging out the underwear I hid under my pile of clothes. Because I'll let her inside my body, but heaven forbid the doctor sees my striped bikini-cut briefs. I roll my eyes at myself and step into the panties, pull my maroon shift dress back over my head, and slide my feet into my sandals.

Grabbing my phone, I see my sisters are still active in our group chat. They're back home in Idaho attending State College, but these dummies are my best friends, and since I graduated last year, I miss them so hard it hurts.

Me: *No real answers from the doc. She's giving me a cream. There's also a shot I can try, but it's elective. And crazy expensive. Guess it's time to try that dumb toy.*

Mads: *I have high hopes for you. My roommate says the Petal Pulverizer is "life-changing." That's a direct quote. And for what they're charging for the thing, it better take you to the moon and back AND make you breakfast in the morning.*

She's right, the toy was also expensive. All of my spare cash this year is going toward this self-pleasure side quest, and the lack of success is maddening. I wish I could follow the common advice to "stop trying so hard to reach the destination and learn to enjoy the journey," but that would require me to turn off my entire personality. I try hard. It's who I am. Normally my efforts produce results, like getting a good enough LSAT score to make it into Franklin Monroe. But all my trying seems to mean nothing when it comes to making my body cooperate.

Me: *We'll see. I'm not getting my hopes up.*

Our youngest sister finally chimes in.

Mandy: *When you decide you hate this toy as much as all the others, bring it to the wedding so I can take it off your hands.*

I sigh at her mention of the wedding. I've always been close with all three of my siblings, but my relationship with our older brother is…complicated. I love Mike. I do. And I also love his fiancée, Danielle, and the rest of her crazy family. I wouldn't miss their wedding for the world. But our family history is hard. Mike's doing well now, he worked hard to get where he is. But watching your big brother go to rehab three times for addiction to prescription narcotics takes a toll, and big life events like this now come with lots of extra feelings.

At least our younger sisters get me. Even though they can also drive me nuts, which Mandy especially delights in doing. (Yes, all the Miller children have first names starting with the letter M. People might call me Shelley, but it's short for Michelle.)

Me: *What is wrong with you? Repeat after me. We do not ask for used vibrators.*

Mandy: *Sorry for caring about the environment and trying to reduce consumer waste. I'll sanitize it, obviously. What's the point of letting it rot in your drawer?*

Me: *Stop! And who says I won't like it? Maddy's roommate says it's life-changing, remember?*

Spoiler alert: Life-changing it is not.

Back in my apartment, as expected, I can't do it. Just like every other time, nothing happens. It's been almost forty minutes of attempting to stimulate myself with this flower-shaped mini vacuum, and I'm getting sore and chafed, so I give up. My body is broken, and it doesn't matter how many times or how many different ways I try, I'm never going to be able to get there. The Petal Pulverizer toy lying next to me is just the latest in a long line of failed gadgets, not to mention a waste of one hundred eighty-seven dollars. Which, since I'm living off student loans at the moment, is money I'll be paying back in interest for years.

I pull a pillow over my face and scream in frustration before I take the toy and throw it at my closet, but because I can't do anything right today, it falls short and lands softly on the carpet.

Could this be any more humiliating?

Me: *Epic fail. Petal remains unpulverized.*

I send one last text to the sister group chat and absentmindedly scroll up through the thread. Seeing the photo of Jo's article from earlier gives me an idea. If anyone I know might have a valid, scientific opinion about what's going on with me, it will be my old teammate. I should reach out to her, right?

Yes. I can do this.

Before I chicken out, I create a new memo in my voice recording app.

Hi, Jo. It's Shelley Miller. I have an awkward question for you. I know it's been a while since we've talked, but I'm following your work and cheering you on from the sidelines. I saw your article this morning in my doctor's office. The one that said up to fifteen percent of women have never, um, achieved a climax? Uh, well, I think, or I should say I **know** *I'm in that* *camp, unfortunately. And I'm just wondering if you have any, like, professional advice for people in my…situation? I already see a few doctors on the regular. I don't know what's wrong with me or my body, other than it might be a side effect of my ADHD meds, and I would love to finally get an answer. Do you think we might be able to chat when you have a free minute? Sorry, I know this is awkward. Thanks for considering.*

I take a breath and gather my courage, then type "Jo" into the search area. It brings up my J contacts, and I click her name quickly to send the message, then I slam my phone face-down on the bed.

Just breathe. It's a medical problem. Nothing wrong with seeking an opinion from a professional.

It's not long before the phone buzzes. I swallow and take another calming breath, trying to force myself to be mature about this whole thing.

The plan to act like an adult immediately goes out the window when I see the message is from my brother's best friend.

Jordan: *Hey, Shelley. I think you intended this for someone else.*

Chapter 2

Shelley

My stomach drops straight through my feet.

No.

No no no no no. This cannot be happening.

I sent that message to Jordan? Not Josephine Wilson? But Jordan Freaking Wagner?

As in my professional baseball-playing brother's best friend and teammate. The guy Mike currently lives with, and the one on whom I've been secretly crushing since the first time we met. That Jordan? The one with the great smile who makes the most intense eye contact I've ever experienced. Jordan just heard me say out loud in my own voice that I can't climax. Plus, now he knows I need to see a psychiatrist on a regular basis.

Awesome.

Me: *Sorry. I can't respond to you right now because my soul left my body and I have expired.*

Jordan: *OK. R.I.P. But it's sad knowing you're gone before you ever really lived.*

Me: *OMG. Stop. Can we please pretend this never happened?*

My phone rings. It's him. Great. Just what I need today.

"So much for pretending," I answer.

"If that's what you want, that's fine. But before I let it go, I feel a responsibility to say you don't need to be embarrassed about this."

I scoff. "Okay, great. Let me just switch off my human emotions tap, since you're the one deciding how I feel now. Turn the embarrassment off, you say? Perfect. All better now. Why didn't I think of that?" Do I feel a little bit bad about snapping at him? Sure. But he still doesn't get to tell me how to react.

"Sorry. I only meant you're probably not the problem in this scenario."

I scoff again, harder this time. If there were any weight to that theory, the Petal Pulverizer would have proven itself more effective, and I'd be blissed out and sinking into a three-hour nap instead of having this conversation or considering injections.

"Maybe your partner just doesn't know what they're doing?" he offers.

Can someone please tell me where men get their audacity? They seem to buy it in bulk.

"Not helping. Also, that assumes there is a partner," I counter.

There's a smile behind the words when he says, "Fair point, Counselor. I see why they let you into law school."

I should not be talking to my brother's friend about this. He's not a doctor. He's the starting first baseman for the North Bay Blue Crabs, the minor league team in a tiny little waterfront town in the Northern Neck of Virginia. Outside of the few times I visited Mike and Jordan was nice to me, we hardly know each other. So what if he's tall, kind of funny, and seems to be trying to be sweet in a misguided, but well-meaning sort of way? None of that gives him the right to weigh in on my sex life. Or lack thereof. I clearly did not invite him into this discussion on purpose.

There's a long pause before he speaks again. "Do you want to know what I think?"

Is he for real? "Here we go. Let me guess what happens next. This is the part where you offer to snake my drain and fix all my problems, right?"

I don't care if Mike will be mad if I'm rude to his friend. After the day I've had, I'm fresh out of tolerance for bros who offer up their bodies like the obvious solution. If Jordan's going to be one of them, then my brother's best friend is about to get his ass handed to him.

Every guy I've dated since I started college has been convinced he'll be the one with the magic wand and the ability to solve the calculus problem between my legs. They're always wrong. But because this is Jordan, and *maybe* I've always harbored a small, tiny, *minuscule* crush on him, now I'm also a little bit curious. But mostly insulted. What does he think he knows that I haven't been able to figure out about my own body with a team of doctors?

He laughs, interrupting my thoughts. "No thanks. Also? Knowing you've been hanging out with guys who say things like 'snake your drain' only confirms my theory."

"It wasn't an invitation," I grind out.

Apparently, this *can* get more embarrassing. That was a pretty swift rejection, not that I blame him for setting boundaries. I'm the one who asked, and also the one accidentally dragging him into this.

Still, my ego is thankful when he's quick to clarify, "Nothing against you. I don't hook up during the season anyway, but even if I did, your brother would kick my ass just for having this conversation. Teammates' sisters are off-limits. But if the doctors don't see a reason, I'm just saying, you're probably overthinking this."

I bristle at the accusation, even though it's the same thing multiple medical professionals have told me. The no sex thing on his part is new information. Look at us learning all kinds of new stuff about each other today. Although, I'm not exactly surprised he has a quirk about stuff interfering with his baseball season. From what Mikey's told me, I already know Jordan, like a lot of other athletes, is superstitious about not shaving and following strict routines. Only now he seems to be admitting a razor isn't the only thing he hasn't touched since spring training started. Interesting.

But he's also not wrong. We shouldn't go there.

"I get it. Although, the future attorney in me feels compelled to point out Mike isn't your teammate anymore, so the sisters rule no longer applies. Anyway, we can go straight to the pretending this didn't happen now."

My brother has been recruited by the new Virginia Foxhounds team. He's moving up to the major league, so technically they are no longer teammates. But Jordan is also my brother's best man, which probably means the bro code is still in effect, and definitely means we'll be seeing each other at the wedding soon. As if we needed a way to make this whole situation even more uncomfortable. Hopefully we can put this little glitch of a conversation behind us by then.

I can hear the smirk in his voice. "The Keep-Hands-Off-Sisters Policy has no expiration date. But like I said, don't be embarrassed about the voicemail. It's not a big deal. We're cool."

"I'm trying." I sigh. "Thanks for not being a jerk about the whole thing."

"Literally the very least I can do."

Maybe he has a point. The bar is on the ground if I'm thanking a guy just for not being a jerk. I need to raise my standards.

"Okay, true. But I still appreciate it. And I'm sorry I snapped at you. It was actually nice of you to try to make me feel better," I reluctantly admit.

"Did it work?"

"Maybe a little." A tiny smile forms on my face. "Thanks."

"Sure. Have a good night."

"Hey, Jordan?" I chew on my bottom lip for a few seconds while a dangerous new idea plants itself in my mind.

"Yeah?"

I don't know if I should say what I want to ask. I'm sure it crosses several lines, but it's been hard to get a guy's perspective on this issue. It's not like I can ask Mike or our dad for advice here. And every time I try to broach the subject with someone I date, they immediately want to hop into bed with me and prove themselves. I know Jordan won't do that. He's already made it abundantly clear he doesn't want me. While the thought stings my pride a bit, it also makes him a neutral sounding board. This is the first time I've been able to talk to a man I trust and know he's not going to try to get in my pants as soon as I mention it.

Here goes nothing.

"Believe it or not, it did help to hear you say that stuff. Sorry if this is too much. Feel free to say no, but for my own sanity I need to ask you something."

"Okay…"

I take a deep breath and launch into my proposal. "Do you think you'd be open to talking to me more about things like this sometime? From a completely platonic male friend perspective? Platonic being the key word." He's quiet on the other end of the line, so I continue rambling. "I swear I'm not asking you to get horizontal with me. I'm just realizing I really do need to talk about this with someone who's not related to me. My sisters do what they can, but it's not the same. Not like it would be with you."

Somebody needs to take this phone away from me. Seriously.

Eventually, he speaks. "I really should say no to that."

It doesn't escape me that he didn't.

"But?"

I wrap my blanket around my shoulders and put him on speakerphone, so his smooth, deep voice fills my room.

"Shelley. Look, I don't know how appropriate it is to talk to you about this. I'm a lot older than you, and you're still my buddy's little sister. I do consider you a friend, but I'm not trying to do anything that comes between you and Mike or screws up my own friendship with your brother."

"You won't," I protest. "I'm only looking for someone I can trust to be honest with me and not get creepy."

He blows out a long breath. "I can promise I'm not going to initiate any more conversations about this. At all. So, if after this conversation you still want to pretend tonight never happened, we can do that. No hard feelings." I hear him shift his body. "All kidding aside, I'm sure it took a lot of courage for you to ask, and your first message sounded kind of serious. That's why I called you in the first place. If you're looking into professional help, then this is obviously a real issue for you. I'm not sure what I'll be able to do, but if you have questions and you think I can offer any insight, I'll answer you. Okay? That's the best I can do."

His measured, thoughtful response is somehow both incredibly frustrating and exactly what I needed to hear, even though the words are still mostly a rejection. I wonder if he would give the same careful answer to any other friend. Is he only hesitating because he knows my brother? Jordan isn't really much older than I am, I think he's only twenty-eight. A six-year age gap is hardly scandalous when both parties are fully grown. But I do appreciate him trying to do the right thing, even if his sense of loyalty to Mike is a little misguided and outdated. At least he's willing to be a sounding board, and a guy friend I can be real with sounds like it could be exactly what I need.

"Sounds fair. Thanks."

"Sure. Goodnight."

"Night."

Like I'm going to be able to get any sleep now.

Chapter 3

Jordan

"Give me three more," Robin orders. When I glare at her, the team's physical therapist only laughs and shakes her head.

My arms burn, and I sneak a glance at the clock. We're nearing the end of my P.T. session, and I'm trying to think about anything except my damn elbow, which hasn't been the same since I injured it last season.

She taps her fitness watch, a not-so-subtle signal for me to hurry up and finish my last set of bicep curls. "Come on, some of us have wives and children to get home to."

"Sure, rub it in." I flash her my best smile, but she's immune. I briefly consider asking for advice about Shelley, but quickly realize it would probably only earn me a one-way ticket to a meeting with H.R.

Hell if I know whether that was the right way to respond last night, but it's not like there was anyone I could ask when her message came through. Mike's the only friend I might feel remotely comfortable talking to about this sort of thing, but I'm not about to approach the guy and ask him to press pause on his wedding plans so he can offer me advice on how to help his sister handle her orgasm problem. At least not if I want to keep all my teeth.

Robin narrows her eyes. "Focus. You're stuck in your head today. That's how injuries happen."

"Three. Two. One," I grunt out the countdown and set down the forty-pound dumbbells before taking a seat on the weight bench. It's been a year since I took that hit, but weight exercises still pinch in a way I never felt before I went down.

"How did this set feel?"

"Fine," I lie.

Robin's brow arches, calling my bluff.

Trying not to focus on the dull, radiating pain in my arm, I let my mind drift back to the message that came out of nowhere. I was surprised to see Shelley's name pop up on my screen. We've always been friendly, but we don't see each other often, only the few times a year when she visits her brother. I probably should've stopped listening and deleted her message after the first sentence. It was clear she sent it to me accidentally. But it felt like something that deserved a response.

Voices rise in the hall, and I glance up toward the doorway. Our new shortstop is walking with our pitcher, Lincoln, in the direction of Coach Johnson's office.

"Did you get a chance to talk to Beau yet?" Robin's voice cuts into my thoughts again as she tries to make conversation.

I shrug and wipe the sweat from my face with a towel. "Not really."

Coach brought the rookie into the locker room yesterday, where Beauchamp insisted in his trademark Southern drawl we all call him Beau. We acknowledged him with nods and polite hellos, but I haven't gone out of my way to introduce myself to our new shortstop. He seems like a decent guy, if maybe a bit overconfident, but the reality is we only need a new shortstop because Miller's gone. I'd rather not focus too much on the gaping hole my best friend is leaving in my life as he moves up to the majors and out of the apartment we share. Mike's out there living the dream, getting recruited by the Virginia Foxhounds and marrying Danielle.

I, on the other hand, am stagnant. I'm sitting here in the exact same weight room where I've started spring training for the past four years in a row. Only this year I'm not performing as well as I usually do. I have no idea if I'll still be here this time next year, and if I'm not, I have no clue what my other options are. I don't have any real skills outside of the ball field. I didn't have anything else to fall back on, so I never allowed myself to think about a Plan B. But now I'm staring right down the barrel into the bleak probability of needing one.

Robin seems as done with this session as I am, and she calls an end to it five minutes early. "That's enough for today. Put some ice on the elbow when you get home, if you need it. You're still favoring that arm. Come back tomorrow ready to get your head in the game."

I nod and head over to the locker room to shower and change. Robin's right. I'm too lost in my own thoughts, and it could hurt the team tomorrow if I don't snap out of it. But the questions about myself I try to avoid have been lingering in the back of my mind since Shelley brought them all back to the surface last night. If she does try to reach out again, I don't know how to help. How am I supposed to comfort anyone else about their life or their sexuality when I still don't have a solid grasp on my own? I'll be thirty in less than two years. I really thought I would have my shit more together than this by now.

The frustration of a lackluster training session combined with overthinking about that message is messing with me. Unwelcome, complicated feelings swirl in my head as I finish my shower. Turning off the water, I grab a towel and dry off, then I swipe on some deodorant and throw on a Blue Crabs tee and a pair of athletic shorts.

When I head back into the locker room, Lincoln and Rodriguez are there with Beauchamp, gathering their things. I nod at them and grab my bag, ready to leave.

"We were thinking of taking the rookie out to Marnock tonight to grab some drinks and try to score with the ladies, you in?" Lincoln asks.

"You know he's not," Rodriguez says before I have a chance to respond. "He's in full chastity mode until we make the playoffs." He elbows Beauchamp and explains, "Jordan takes the same vow every year."

My teammates think I'm superstitious about remaining celibate during the season, and that's fair enough because I do like to stick to my rituals. But if I'm being honest, it's easier to play along with their assumption than to explain the truth. I don't want to deal with other people's judgments about my life. If Shelley calls again, I'll do what I promised and try to answer her, but I doubt anything I say can make any kind of difference.

"Yeah, I'm out. Don't have too much fun, Rookie. We have a game tomorrow." I put on a hat and give them a two-finger salute as I leave.

When I get home, Mike's sitting on the floor of our living room taping up moving boxes. He greets me with a grunt. I nod and shove my gear into the small coat-closet-slash-pantry. Our apartment's front door opens right into our kitchen, with the tiny living area on the other side of the island. I lean against the counter and stare down at my friend.

"How's the packing going?"

"It's taking forever, but it's fine."

"Do we have any of that soup left from The Blue Crab? I'm starving."

Mike shrugs, so I head to the fridge to check for myself. Thankfully, there is still a little bit in there. I pour a bowl and cover it with a paper towel before I pop it in the microwave. Then I turn back to him. "You need help with these boxes tonight?"

"Nah, I got it." He sits up straight and runs a hand through his hair while he looks at me. I know that face. He wants something. "Can I ask you a different favor, though? It's a big one."

Called it.

"Depends what it is. No way I'm agreeing outright. The last time you asked me this question we ended up singing a duet in the Brew-Ha-Ha Valentine's Day karaoke contest." There was way too much choreography involved, and I had to wrap a sheet around me like a diaper and shoot foam arrows at the audience while pretending to be Cupid. "I'm not falling for an ask like that again."

"Fair." He nods and resumes closing the packed box in front of him while he says, "There's a change in the Foxhounds' schedule. I need to travel to New York a few days before the wedding." The packing tape squeaks as he drags it across the cardboard before adding, "But the Crabs are off that Thursday."

"I know. I'm on Best Man duty for the whole week. You want me to pick up the rings or something? Just tell me what you need, man." How hard can a wedding errand be?

Mike takes a breath and looks up at me again, setting the tape down on top of the box. "Could you drive out to D.C. and pick up Michelle after her morning class lets out?"

I drum my fingers on the counter. "Nobody else is available?" I wince at myself as his face pinches. He looks like a kicked puppy. Note to self, maybe sharing a digital calendar with my roommate wasn't the best idea. He knows I'm free, and I have no realistic excuse to offer, but hours alone with his sister right after she asked me if I'd mentor her about her sex questions seems like an epically bad plan. I know I pissed her off with my first response, then her second set of questions left me spinning out for my own reasons.

"Shelley doesn't have a car," he pleads. Of course she doesn't. She doesn't need one in the city. But it's not like there is any public transit that comes all the way out to North Bay, and hiring a car to drive that far would be insanely expensive. Somebody needs to get her. "Danielle and her crew have wedding stuff to do here in town all week. The rest of my family is flying into Richmond on Friday. They're renting a car, and they did say they could go up and get her, then make the drive back down here, but…"

"That wouldn't make a ton of sense," I concede.

"Exactly, it would be asking my parents to do hours of driving in the wrong direction after a cross-country flight. And if their flight is delayed at all it will screw up the whole plan."

He's right. Washington D.C. traffic is notoriously bad. Plus, we're supposed to get some pretty big storms rolling through over the next few days. The ten-day forecast says the weather should clear up by the end of the week in time for the wedding, but if anything veers off schedule, even slightly, it could derail things for his whole family. Someone does need to go pick up Shelley before the rest of his family gets in, and it's pretty obvious that person should be me.

Mike looks at me, the guilt seeping out of his pores. He knows this road trip will take up my entire day. It's a three-hour drive from North Bay to D.C. in each direction on a good day.

I feel a slow burn spreading up the back of my neck as a bead of sweat rolls down my spine. I should probably fess up and tell him what happened, but then again, Shelley's medical secrets aren't mine to share. Besides, it's not like I acquired this knowledge on purpose. And who wants to hear details like that about their siblings?

"Yeah. I'll get her. No big deal." What's a little road trip trapped in the car with my best friend's sister and her sex questions? I can survive a few hours.

Mike lets out a long, relieved breath. "Thanks, man. That's huge."

I graze my bottom lip with my teeth and turn to take the soup out of the microwave, testing a spoonful to see if it's warm enough.

"We have hotel rooms booked for my family on Friday and through the weekend. But do you think she could sleep here Thursday night?" he adds.

I spit the soup in my mouth down the front of my shirt. He wants her to sleep here, too? While he's out of town?

"You okay?"

"Yep. Soup's a little hot. Sure. That's fine." It comes out squeakier than I intended, and I fake a cough to clear my throat while

I clean up my mess with a paper towel. Then I take an ice pack out of the freezer and cradle it in my elbow while I pick up my bowl again. Apparently, Shelley and I are having a sleepover in my apartment. "I'm going to eat in my room. I'm tired."

Mike nods as he wrestles with another box. "Okay. I'm going to head over to Danielle's with some of these boxes. Or I guess I should call it our house now. See you later."

"Right. I'll see you on the fishing trip, if I don't catch you before then." We have his bachelor party coming up in a few days. I take my soup to the safety of my room before I say too much.

As I settle into bed with my dinner, my phone pings with a new message. My stomach does a little nervous flip, half-expecting to see Shelley's name, but it's from my high school coach. He and his wife, Ruth, like to visit North Bay once a year to watch me play.

Coach Carver: *Can you send me those dates?*

I attach a photo of our team's schedule for the season.

Me: *Here you go. Looking forward to your visit. Say hi to Ms. Ruth. Tell her I miss her oatmeal cookies. Think she'll bring me a batch?*

Coach Carver: *Make your own damn cookies.*

I smile because embracing the grouchy grandpa vibe is the old man's love language. We both know Ms. Ruth will bring me three dozen oatmeal cookies. She always does. The Carvers are nothing if not predictable. They're steady, reliable folks. The only ones I've got, outside of Mike and his parents. Even if the Jordan Wagner fan club is small, having the Carvers in my life means at least once a year there are people in the stands rooting for me.

Me: *Love you, too, Coach.*

Chapter 4

Shelley

"Hahaha! I can't breathe." Madison's wheezing laughter comes through my earbuds as I arrive at the grocery store. The weather is supposed to turn nasty soon, and I want to stock up before the storms come through. I thought talking to my sister would make this shopping trip more pleasant, and it does, her current laughing fit at my expense notwithstanding. But there is so much on my to-do list for today, I'm feeling frazzled, and I know I'll never get to it all. I never do, even though I always seem to be juggling at least two or three things at once.

Mads is practically hyperventilating. "Mikey's making you ride all the way from D.C. to North Bay with Jordan? I bet you're going to prep for this like a deposition, aren't you?"

"Feels more like prepping for a colonoscopy at this point, if I'm being honest."

"Nervous diarrhea?"

"I plead the Fifth."

"You know you're thinking of a list of interview questions for him as we speak." My sister snorts into the phone. "Are you taking a tape recorder? Oh my god, please secretly leave your phone on and let me listen. I'll be so quiet. He'll never know I'm there."

"You're the worst."

"And yet you love me."

"You know what I don't love?" I try to turn the conversation away from Jordan. "That toy you recommended. Total flop."

"Dang. I was really *pulling* for that one. Get it?"

"Ew." My siblings love their stupid puns, but I don't have the patience for any more jokes about this. Especially bad ones. "How's Mandy doing?" I change the subject again.

"Fine. She's loving this for you almost as much as I am."

I should've known better than to tell my sisters about the voice memo fiasco. And what was I thinking asking Jordan if I could approach him with more questions? First, I sent him that message out of the blue, then I snapped at him for trying to comfort me, and then I had the gall to ask him to talk to me about it some more? All of it was beyond inappropriate, and I've been slowly dying of mortification every day since.

Not to be dramatic, but I swear I can feel my insides eroding as the embarrassment deteriorates my esophagus from within. I wish I could blame it on my impulsivity, but I'm pretty sure that whole situation was just Shelley Miller being Shelley Miller.

Jordan and I haven't spoken since *The Incident*, which has done nothing but force the scenario to replay approximately ten million times in my head so I can fixate on all the places where I went wrong. And now Mike wants me to share a night in his old apartment with his best man? Alone. By ourselves. With no one else. Which is what *alone* means.

"Stop ruminating," my sister says since I've gone quiet. "It was one accidental message. He probably hasn't even thought about it."

I grab a cart from the corral, dropping the empty fruit tray I need to return into the carriage, and push it through the automatic doors. "Ugh. That might be worse."

I don't know why. On paper, Jordan not caring at all seems like the best possible outcome. We would never need to discuss it again, and my embarrassment could slowly fade away with time. It's not like I see him very often. But for reasons I can't explain, I hate the idea of something affecting so much of my life meaning nothing to Jordan. I don't want to be forgettable. Especially to him.

Which is stupid. We hardly know each other.

Although, not knowing much about the kind and mysterious first baseman who used to live with my brother hasn't stopped my inconvenient crush on him from taking root. It's only grown since the first time I visited North Bay. So maybe I don't exactly hate the idea of having a little bit of alone time with him, even if it is going to be mortifying.

Thankfully, Madison restrains herself from making any more comments, but I can still picture her eyes rolling from all the way across the country.

"Tell me how Greek life is treating you." I try yet again to change the subject.

She takes the bait this time, launching into the latest gossip about the girls who share her house. I peruse the aisles while she talks, tossing my favorite yogurt and granola bars into the cart until one of her sorority sisters calls out to her and she needs to go. After we say goodbye, I head over to the deli.

"Here you go, Ms. Miller. You sure do throw a lot of parties." The worker behind the counter recognizes me and hands me my special-order catering tray.

I place it carefully in the cart and hand over the empty one from last week. "Call me Shelley. I'm afraid it's a party of one."

He gives me a look I can't interpret. I'm not sure if it's pity, judgment, or just indifference. Sometimes I have a hard time with faces.

I know it's a little unusual to custom order a party-sized fruit and veggie tray every week when I'm the only one eating it, but it's one way I've learned to manage my quirks. Having healthy foods already washed, prepped, and ready to eat keeps me from noshing on takeout every night or forgetting to eat altogether, and saves me money in the long run. It's an accommodation I'm willing to make for myself, but not everyone understands. Or maybe the deli worker couldn't possibly care less and I'm reading too much into it.

Either way, the interaction reminds me I need to put a call in to my psychiatrist for a refill on my meds. And I also still should try to talk to Jo, if I can manage to remember how phones work this time. I wish I didn't have to spend so much of my already limited time dealing with this problem. I've been using the cream Dr. Dupree recommended, and I think I might be noticing a small difference, but not enough to conclude it's working. Is there really no better option than messing with the med schedule it took years to work out?

"Thank you," I tell the deli worker before I push the cart toward the checkout, trying to convince myself that it doesn't matter if he's judging me. As my mom is fond of saying, *what other people think of me is none of my business*.

My phone vibrates with a text I assume is from my sister wanting to share another piece of Theta gossip she forgot. When I see Jordan's name instead, a singular little butterfly dances in my stomach.

Jordan: *Is early afternoon OK to pick you up on Thursday? Mike says the plan is for you to stay here with me for one night, then go to the hotel the next day.*

Me: *Yep. I was also told that's the plan. Thank you for driving me.*

Jordan: *Sure thing.*

There's no logical reason for the smile that finds its way to my face each time a text from him comes through. It will most likely be a long, awkward car ride followed by a quiet night in, with both of us doing our best to talk about anything but my ridiculous question. Okay, questions. Plural.

Still, it means hours alone with one of the most attractive men I've ever met. These days, I need to take my excitement where I can get it.

All the way back to my apartment, my heart dances with anticipation at the same time my stomach gurgles with anxiety and unanswered questions. This crush is really freaking inconvenient. I don't have time to be daydreaming about a baseball player who lives three hours away. I have actual important things to do. Like pass my classes.

At least the spring semester is wrapping up soon, and I'll have a small reprieve before the summer session. And I get to fly home to visit my family during the week-long break in our schedule next month. My mom wants us all to go to the Foxhounds game when Mike's new team plays in Idaho.

As I walk in the door, I kick off my shoes and set my purse on the floor. I toss my keys onto the counter and eye the stack of unopened mail. I'll get to it later. Probably. Come to think of it, I haven't been down to my mail slot for a while either.

After putting the groceries mostly away, I strip out of my fitted jeans and the button-down top I've been wearing all day and kick them toward the in-unit stackable washer and dryer in my hall closet. Which reminds me, I never switched the load I put in yesterday, so now I have to run it again to get out the wet clothes funk. Slipping on some pajama shorts from the full basket of clean clothes that never make it to my drawers and letting the rest of the day melt away, I let out a moan as I unhook my bra and replace it with my Stacy Haverson tank top. Then I drop into a kitchen chair and start my homework before I get sidetracked again.

I get in two solid hours of reading before my eyes cross and the words on the laptop screen are blurry. Taking my computer to my room, I call it a wrap on the studying and open a new tab. It's time to treat myself to a much-needed night in watching the Wing Warriors competition.

When I'm stressed out, which is pretty much always, I like to watch competitive eating challenges. Especially the female competitors. There's something invigorating about seeing a woman dominate a man twice her size by taking down twenty pounds of chicken wings while he taps out next to her. I'm obsessed with Stacy Haverson, the reigning champion.

Flopping onto the nest of pillows in my bed, I set up my computer in front of me. A few seconds later, Stacy's sauce-covered face fills the screen. Now I wish I had chicken wings or something else loaded with sodium and grease. Sparing a glance toward the kitchen, I heave a huge sigh because, despite *just* buying all that prepared food for this exact situation, I know I won't be eating any of it tonight. Why is it so hard to make yourself eat all the healthy things after you bring them home?

It takes approximately thirty seconds for me to cave and place a delivery order for a burger, then I'm able to get lost in the controlled chaos of the event as Stacy tears into a pile of wings, stripping the meat from the bones like the beast she is. With a minute and fourteen seconds left and barbecue sauce coating her neon pink fingernails, she sticks out her tongue to prove she swallowed the final bite.

"Yes!" I jump out of bed and throw my arms in the air, but when I realize I'm screaming alone in my apartment, I quickly bring them down again. Maybe I should get a cat or something. It's lonely not having anyone to share these moments with.

Chapter 5

Jordan

Things in North Bay have been so busy, today sort of snuck up on me, but I'm on my way to get Shelley. After Mike's awkward bachelor party and the crazy storms that caused our games to get cancelled and sent the whole town into a frenzy, Thursday came quickly, even though there was no baseball. At least I got a new roommate out of it. I talked with Danielle's friend, Jake Gibson, at the party, and he's going to move into Mike's old room, along with his bulldog, Hazel.

Jake seems cool, but he definitely has a misguided idea about what's going on between me and Shelley after seeing her latest panic text, which happened to come through while he was putting his number into my phone. Because of course it did. Keeping with her theme of unfortunate messages, that one said, *No one at this wedding can know you have intimate knowledge of my body. I'm serious, Jordan. Promise me.* I told him nothing happened between us, but who would believe me after seeing that?

After three and a half hours in the car, the last thirty minutes of which were spent in a two-mile long construction detour, I finally make it to the street in front of Shelley's apartment. It's a red brick student housing unit that looks a little worn down, but the surrounding neighborhood seems nice, judging by the community playground and cafes with bistro tables on the sidewalks. I want to walk up to her door to get her, but there doesn't seem to be anywhere to park. As I circle the block at a snail's pace for the second time, a tap on the passenger window startles me. Shelley opens the back door as I slam on the brakes, and she tosses in her suitcase. The car was hardly moving, so the actual act of stopping isn't as dramatic as the thumping in my chest makes it feel.

"Jesus. You scared me. Do you still have all your toes over there?"

"All little piggies intact. Thanks for doing this," Shelley says as she climbs into the front seat. The car behind us honks, and she turns around and smiles, flashing them a peace sign, which makes me laugh.

"No problem."

The click of her seatbelt echoes through the car, and I maneuver my way back onto the crowded streets. An uncomfortable silence tries to settle over us, but I clear my throat, not wanting to let it.

"Have you had lunch yet? I wouldn't mind making a pit stop."

"Sorry. I should've thought to invite you up, but I know parking around here is a nightmare."

"It's all good. But are you hungry?"

"I can always eat." She shrugs. "Burgers? They're my favorite. I know a pretty great little local shop hidden out of the way."

"That works."

She directs me down some side roads, and we find street parking in a back alley just a few buildings down from the tiny shack serving food out of its front window. It looks like someone converted an old shed stuck between two townhouses. I follow her lead, and we stand close together waiting for our turn to order. There's a line of about a dozen people ahead of us, but it's moving quickly.

"I should warn you, they only have one option. It's a three-pack of sliders, and they don't take custom orders, so you have to take it or leave it. But trust me, as long as you don't mind diced onion, they're fantastic," Shelley tells me.

It already smells amazing. "That's cool, I'm not picky. I'm sure whatever we're about to get will be infinitely better than some of the struggle meals I've forced down over the years."

She nods and says, "I think you'll like these. I'm a little bit picky about other things, but not food. My favorite competitive eater came here once and ate forty-three of these little burgers in an hour. I've never been able to eat more than six." The disappointment in her voice makes me chuckle at her admission.

"Six is still pretty impressive," I reassure her, and she shrugs.

It's refreshing how Shelley is so unapologetically herself. I should've known today wouldn't be a problem. She's easy to be around, and she makes me laugh.

"I don't think I would've pegged you as a competitive eater, but I have to say, I'm intrigued," I say.

"Oh, I'm nowhere close to competitive, just a spectator. But I love watching it. Especially Stacy Haverson. There's something so fascinating about people pushing their bodies to the limit. I guess it's true for any sport, but I like that it's something just about anyone with any body type can train themselves to do. You don't need fancy equipment or expensive trainers." Her face lights up while she talks, and she's so animated that she needs to pause to take a deep breath after her sentence before launching into another one.

She goes on, "Imagine a woman who is like five-foot-two. She might never have a shot at the NBA, but she absolutely could train her body to take on any one of those same seven-foot-tall guys in an eating competition. And she could win. It evens out everyone in terms of endurance, level of play, et cetera." Her golden hair is pulled up into a high ponytail that bounces as she speaks, using her hands for emphasis. It's kind of cute.

There's a small smile forming on my face as I listen, but inwardly I remind myself I shouldn't be looking at her like this.

"I think I get it." I nod. "I do like the idea that the effort someone put into their training is more important than the body they were born into. When it comes to baseball, I can train as much as I want, but I still might never measure up to someone who was born with a taller, leaner body, better eyesight, and more natural talent. You're saying this is more of a level playing field."

"Exactly."

"Maybe I should train for competitive eating after I'm done with baseball?"

"Yeah? Let me know when that happens, and I'll take you on." She nudges me playfully.

We find ourselves at the front of the line, and Shelley orders two packages and two sodas to go. She pulls out her wallet, but I step in and hand over the cash before she can take out her card. Shelley gives me a quizzical look, but when I subtly shake my head at her, she seems to accept that I'm not taking no for an answer on this one.

If I have an opportunity to feed someone, I'm always going to do it. That's not negotiable for me. There was a long time in my life when I had no choice but to rely on the generosity of the people around me. Back then I promised myself that when I grew up, whenever I was in the position to be the one providing a meal for someone, I always would.

The cashier hands over a greasy paper bag. We didn't order them, but apparently we didn't have to, because every order also comes topped with a scoop of loose French fries.

"Thank you for lunch," Shelley says as we head back to my car. "You really didn't have to do that. I'm already putting you out by crashing at your place. I'll pay for gas, and I've got dinner later."

Other than another shake of my head, I chose to ignore her last comment and launch back into our previous discussion. "So, that's why you like Stacy Haverson? The athleticism?"

Shelley opens the bag to take out a fry and pops it in her mouth while she gives me an impressed look. There's already a second fry in her hand, which she points at me when she says, "You remember her name."

I'm not sure why she seems surprised. "Of course I remember, you just told me like three minutes ago. Plus, it's not every day my closest friend's own sister passes over both of us to choose someone else as her favorite athlete," I tease.

"Just don't ask me to pick a favorite baseball player." She nudges my shoulder again before plucking more fries out of the bag, and a tiny jolt of adrenaline runs through me at the contact. "You might not like the answer. Miller sibling loyalties run deep. I'm contractually obligated to say it's Mike," Shelley jokes back.

"I see how it is." I grab the bag from her and jog around to my side of the car. "See if you get these back now."

She laughs that deep belly laugh again, and it lights her up from the inside, turning her into a beam of magnetic sunshine. As she slides into her seat, her bike shorts roll up a bit higher on her thigh, and I look away quickly so she doesn't get the wrong impression. Shelley pretends to pout and turns to me with wide, exaggerated eye contact while she points toward the bag in my lap. I cave immediately, handing the food back to her. I know I'm in trouble when the thought hits that I should've made her come over here to get the bag for herself. It's been a long time since anyone had me thinking this way.

"Haha. Sucker." She snorts.

I roll my eyes. "Just don't get ketchup on the seats."

"Yes, sir." She's kidding, but my body doesn't know that, and with two little words she reignites a spark that's been dormant for years. Too bad I'm not going to do anything about it.

Chapter 6

Between attending classes and squeezing in medical appointments this semester, I almost forgot what it feels like to have fun. I don't know why I was so nervous about today. Being with Jordan is easy. It's one of the things I like best about him. He has this welcoming energy that invites people to be authentic and have a good time when he's around.

Of course he doesn't bring up my little *issue*, because why would he? Instead, we ride to North Bay with the warm fries sitting on the center console between us, sharing lunch and talking about whatever random things cross our minds.

As we barrel down the highway, Jordan keeps his eyes on the road as he reaches over for the bag, but he misses by an inch and ends up grabbing my hand instead.

"Oh, sorry." He pulls away quickly.

"No problem. I believe you were looking for this?" I hand him a fry. As he eats it, I may or may not be watching his jaw work out of the corner of my eye, even after I turn to face forward again. We make easy conversation and the time flies by. Before I know it, we're pulling into his apartment complex.

Jordan carries my bag and leads the way upstairs. But as soon as we step over the threshold into his apartment, the vibe changes because neither of us knows how we are supposed to act now that we're alone together for the night.

"Uh, Mike's old bed is still set up in his room for you. Jake won't be moving the rest of his furniture here for a few days," he tells me, handing me my suitcase with a stiff outstretched arm, like I've suddenly developed cooties and an extra head, and he doesn't want to get too close.

"Oh. Okay. Great. Thanks."

"Uh-huh."

Silence floats between us. If this were an old Western movie, a tumbleweed would roll by. Hello, awkward, my old friend, I was wondering when you'd show up today.

"I guess I'll just..." I point down the hall and show myself to my brother's almost-completely-empty room. A few boxes, which I assume belong to Jake, are piled in the corner. All of Mike's clothes and other belongings have already been moved. The biggest thing left in this room is the bed, still made up with my brother's sheets and comforter, which thankfully, at least smell like he washed them recently.

I set my stuff down on the floor and sit on the edge of the mattress, already unsure what to do with myself. I feel like I'm invading Jordan's space, and it's only now occurring to me that I don't belong here. Why didn't I just book myself an extra night at the hotel? I mean, sure, my credit cards are already full of doctor co-pay charges, school supplies, and food costs, but I could've made it work. The invitation to stay here tonight wasn't really Mike's to offer.

I'm kicking myself for not realizing it sooner and allowing Mike to put Jordan in this position. And me. My brother does that, though. He's always trying to take care of people, and sometimes he oversteps. I'm glad he finally has his life together, but it's hard not to let my old feelings of resentment creep back in when these things happen. It sure would've been nice to have that kind of brotherly love in my life back when I needed it, rather than now as an adult, when it feels overbearing.

The bedroom door is open, but Jordan still knocks on the frame when he approaches, holding up his phone in the other hand. Mike's face looks back at me from the screen.

"Someone thought he needed to make sure I got you here safely," Jordan explains.

Of course he did. Never mind the fact that I could've found my own way to an out-of-town wedding. I didn't actually need Mike to get involved. It's also a little annoying to feel like I'm just another item on his checklist, something else that needs to be managed this weekend.

I roll my eyes and plaster on an exaggerated smile. "Hi, Mikey. As you can see, your best man accomplished his task." I gesture with one hand up and down my body to prove we arrived in one piece, but there's a little bit more bite than necessary behind my response.

I blow out a breath.

I'm being too hard on my brother. It's his wedding week.

Mike's life was in complete shambles for so long back when he was using, and now he has a thing about making sure situations are under control and the people close to him are okay. Is that really so bad? I know I should try harder to understand, and I *am* trying. But, honestly, who does he think was managing everything with our little sisters back when Mom and Dad were dealing with his drama? Hint: it was me. Over-achieving eldest daughter at your service, everyone.

Still, I love him, and I know he means well.

Mike's oblivious to the conflicting feelings bubbling up in me as he says, "Hey, Shells. Glad you got there in one piece. Sorry I'm not around today. Thanks, Jordan. See you guys tomorrow."

"Yep. Go do your baseball thing. We'll be fine." I wave goodbye to my brother while Jordan hangs up.

Then I stare up at Jordan, and he lets his eyes linger on my face a little longer than feels strictly necessary. I can't tell if his eyes are more brown or green, but there are flecks of gold in the hazel that make his irises look like caramel apples. Warm, sweet, and inviting. His gaze travels down my body quickly, stopping briefly at my cleavage before it lands on the floor, which causes a confused little baby butterfly to try to take flight in my belly once again. Does he like what he sees?

"Want to play a game or something?" he asks, pocketing his phone and bringing his mesmerizing eyes back up to mine again.

"Sure. Do you have Scrabble?"

"Ha. No, but even if I did, I'm not going up against a law student in that one. What was it you said earlier about evening the playing field? We need to stick to games we both have an equal opportunity to win."

I laugh. "Okay, well, barring a wing-eating contest between the two of us, what did you have in mind?"

"Cards Against Humanity?"

"You can't play that with only two people." I tisk.

He smirks at me. "Sure we can. Whoever makes the other person laugh hardest wins the round."

I like that idea. "Oh, you're so on."

We sit at the kitchen island and play for over an hour. When the black card on the counter says *Hey baby, come back to my place and I'll show you [blank]* Jordan puts down a card that reads *a cooler full of organs*.

"Just some friendly advice, maybe save those organs for a second or third date," I tell him. "We ladies like to keep the mystery alive."

"Noted." A half-smile plays with his lips, and his shoulders shake with silent laughter. By the time we've run out of cards, we are both cackling so much my sides hurt. The awkward vibe from earlier is gone.

"I concede," I tell him. "You win."

"Yes! Victory is mine." He shoots his fist into the air, those magic eyes shining brightly at me. "Are you hungry?" he asks, lowering his arm while he glances at the clock on the microwave.

"Of course."

The humor seems to leave his face for the briefest millisecond, but it returns just as quickly. "Let me see what I've got. I'll make us something."

"But I promised to buy you dinner," I argue.

"That won't be necessary. The Blue Crab is the only place to go, and they're closing an hour early every night this week to prep the food for the wedding. Besides, I have stuff here."

Right. Small town. Limited options.

"You cook? I'm impressed."

"Yeah, why? You don't?"

"No. Absolutely not."

"What do you mean? You eat, don't you?"

"Sure. I also have a mean trigger finger that can dial for delivery in seconds. Or I eat things that come fully prepared. Fruit, yogurt, lunch meat, cheese. I can put out some charcuterie like nobody's business."

He chuckles. "That counts. I love charcuterie."

"Of course you do. Everyone loves it." But that's not exactly what I mean. I tend to pick foods based on how many dishes they'll require. "Why dirty a bowl, a whisk, a pan, a plate, and a fork making myself some scrambled eggs when I can pop a bagel in the toaster and eat it over a paper towel? Then I only have to wash the knife I used to spread the cream cheese."

"That just sounds efficient." He shrugs.

"I think so. But if you're looking for a woman who will feed you homemade chicken and dumplings or whatever, I'm not her."

Thankfully, living in the city means I never have to cook. There's always something available, and it usually tastes a lot better than my sad attempts at creating something edible in the kitchen. Although, all the take-out is not helping my credit card bills.

He looks at me for a long moment with an expression I can't place before he says, "I actually know how to make my own chicken and dumplings, so I'm good there. But thanks for looking out."

"Really?" I'm intrigued.

"Yeah, I used to stay with my high school coach and his family sometimes. They wanted me to learn how to be independent. Mrs.

Carver taught me how to cook a few things. She was really big on casseroles and Crock-Pot meals."

"That sounds kind of nice."

"It was." His voice holds the tenderness of the memory. "It was homey."

"I know the feeling. I miss having family dinners with homemade food, laughing with people around the table."

"Me, too."

We might not have a slow cooker at the ready, but it's comfortable and domestic here in his apartment as Jordan sets to work making us a quick stir-fry and I set out plates and silverware.

"Hey, so I thought maybe in the morning I could take you to that coffee and karaoke place and treat you to breakfast before I head over to the hotel. Especially since you fed me all day today," I offer.

Jordan grabs two glasses from the cabinet next to the sink. His shirt rises, and I catch a glimpse of the V-shaped indentation in his obliques, pointing down like a neon flashing arrow straight toward what I know I shouldn't be thinking about. He fills the glasses with water and hands me one before leaning back against the counter to sip his own.

"We can go out tomorrow. But you're not paying."

I roll my eyes. "I can't believe you're one of *those* guys. No, I'm not letting you pay for me again. Sorry to tell you, but women are allowed to have jobs now and everything. We can at least take turns."

His smile doesn't quite reach his eyes anymore when he holds out his glass to clink it against mine.

"I usually just microwave a Toaster Strudel or something in the morning," he admits, taking another sip.

"I'm sorry, you do what?!" I'm appalled. "Who microwaves a Toaster Strudel? It tells you right in the name, they go in the *toaster*."

He shrugs and tosses some pre-chopped frozen vegetables into a pan, along with a spoonful of jarred garlic. "I don't have a toaster."

"Well, this is it. It's finally happening. We've reached a fundamental disagreement. I simply can no longer be your friend. I can't support a life without toast. Think of all those poor untoasted bagels, sandwiches, and Pop-Tarts," I tease.

"Sorry to tell you, but I also eat my Pop-Tarts straight out of the package."

"What?! Blasphemy. I'm pretty sure the toaster is the thing they're supposed to *pop* out of, hence the name." I watch as he adds soy sauce to the veggies and boils water for rice noodles in a separate pot before tossing everything together. It smells like a restaurant in here, and he's only been cooking for ten minutes.

"What can I say? I'm a rebel who willfully ignores the directions on packaged pastries. It's my fatal flaw," Jordan says, plating our food.

I scan him up and down and exaggerate my disappointment as I take a seat for dinner. "I'd rather skip breakfast altogether than let you take me down with you."

He shakes his head at me good-naturedly.

The meal he threw together is amazing. A girl could get used to this. I wonder if I could get him to consider giving up baseball to be my own private chef.

When we're finished, we move the few steps into the living room and sit together on the loveseat watching old sitcom reruns on

TV. A small crocheted baseball with a cute embroidered face stares back at us from on top of the console and makes me smile.

It feels good to let my guard down around him, but when I shift my weight and my arm brushes his, Jordan reminds me exactly how he thinks of me when he scoots away to put more space between us. I'm still just Mike's little sister to him. I probably always will be.

After a few episodes, we say goodnight and retreat into our separate, lonely rooms.

Chapter 7

Shelley

As happy as I am for Mike and Danielle, there's a tiny pang of jealousy as I watch my brother exchange vows with his new bride. They're standing on the decorated pier in the Gibson's yard, overlooking the Chesapeake Bay. I've never felt anything close to the love I can see in their faces when they look at each other.

Rows of white wooden chairs have been placed with precision in the grass. Mrs. Gibson truly outdid herself. The perfectly manicured lawn of her waterfront property looks amazing, and with the big white tent set up for the reception area, it's the perfect wedding venue.

I'm in the reserved seats in the front row, sandwiched between my parents and my sisters, as we face out to the water. My brother and Danielle are under a floral arch at the end of the pier, flanked by the other members of their wedding party. Mike's eyes are locked on his bride, and Danielle is glowing in her white gown. The gentle breeze flows through her hair as he looks at her with adoration. His smile is so wide, it practically reaches his ears. I've never seen him happier.

It seems like all of North Bay is here to witness the wedding. Somehow, Mike has become this town's golden boy. Suddenly, he's the rich professional baseball player who swooped in to win the heart of a local. Everyone here knows him as the stand-up guy who runs Narcotics Anonymous meetings at the library. He's the reason my parents are beaming with pride. But these are all recent developments. It hasn't always been this way. Just a few years ago, he was a total screw-up.

But this day is a celebration, so I shift in my seat and try to push away the other memories with a shake of my head.

Jordan's standing next to my brother, and my eyes wander over to him in that tan suit. When he glances in my direction and catches me staring, I startle hard enough to make Mandy start snickering next to me. I elbow her a little harder than necessary, causing her to grunt, and Dad turns to glare in our direction until we settle down. For the rest of the ceremony, I try to pay attention and ignore the way the unforgiving wooden chair is causing me to feel a dull ache where my tailbone tries to stab its way through the fabric of my dress. It really is a beautiful wedding, though.

Once the formal part of the day is finished and we've moved on to dinner and dancing, I take my seat with my family at a round table under the tent in our hosts' backyard. I don't know why Jake would want to leave this gorgeous place to share a tiny apartment with Jordan, but maybe the way Shelia Gibson is glaring at her son as he dances with Danielle's maid of honor, Alice, is hinting at some family drama there.

Mandy's sitting on my right, and she leans in close to whisper, "Have you talked to your love guru yet today?"

"Oh, I heard they've been doing lots of talking. I bet the sleepover was fun," Mads cuts in from my other side.

"Both of you can bite me," I mumble.

"Sounds like something you should be asking Jordan to do, honestly. I mean, look at the man." Mandy smirks and turns toward him, and I swat her shoulder.

"Don't look, he'll see you!" I growl, but I let myself peek. Somewhere between the ceremony and reception, Jordan lost his tie. Beneath his linen suit jacket the first two buttons of his crisp white shirt are unbuttoned.

"Look at your face." Mandy points at me, waving her index finger in a circle. "You totally want to make smasharoni and cheese with him."

I sigh, exasperated. "What would the cheese even be in that scenario?"

She wiggles her eyebrows, causing me to immediately regret the question.

"You know what? Never mind." I smooth my dress and pretend not to care.

"It's true, though, and you know it. You're jonesin' for a bonin'," Mads quips. When their joint giggle fit hits, I know I've lost them.

"Craving some depraving!"

"Good one. Hankering for a spank..*ering*?"

I roll my eyes while they double over laughing at their own ridiculous rhymes. Then I poke them both hard in their ribs.

Mom smiles at us and leans across the table. "Ooh, what are we whispering about over here?"

"Nothing," Mads and I say together, while Mandy betrays me and tells her, "Shelley thinks Jordan's hot."

Mom nods knowingly. "I'm sure you aren't alone in that, Sweetie. He's very handsome, isn't he? Why don't you go ask him to dance? He's just right over there." She extends her arms and motions toward where Jordan is standing with several of his teammates.

"Mom! For the love of everything sacred, please do not point at him," I beg.

Then my mother does what she does best and goes yet another step too far with her meddling. "Jordan!" she calls. "Yoohoo! Come over here and say hello to the mother of the groom. We haven't seen you all evening."

He smiles at her and starts walking toward our table while I groan and sink further in my seat, trying to disappear.

"*Thirsty?*" Mandy asks me, as she refills my water glass with a knowing smirk.

I kick her shin under the table.

When Jordan reaches us, my mom stands and wraps him in a tight hug. She loves him for the way he immediately took my brother under his wing when Mike first moved to North Bay. As far as she's concerned, Jordan's part of our family. I straighten up again, extra-aware of my posture.

"So good to see you, how are you doing these days without Mikey attached at your hip?" Mom asks, as though it hasn't been less than a week since my brother vacated the apartment they shared. Before Jordan has a chance to answer, she keeps talking. "Have you tried the cupcakes yet? I heard there's a story there."

Jordan laughs. "Yeah, Danielle's friends Jake and Alice went to pick up the cupcakes the day the storm hit. They were trapped together for three days. Now they're looking pretty cozy together." He tilts his head in their direction.

"Jake Gibson? Mikey said he's planning to take over the room in your apartment."

"Sure is. He's already moved some of his things."

My mother clasps her hands in front of her. "That's wonderful. I hated thinking of you in that apartment all alone. You know, you should come out to visit us in Idaho soon. I'm trying to organize a trip for the family to see Mikey's game when the Foxhounds come to town. Have you ever been out West? I hope you'll consider joining us." Mom's eyes drift over to me. "Anyway, I was just telling Shelley how nice you all look tonight and how much I love her dress. Don't you just love it?" She reaches out to take my hand, laying it on thick. "Truly, dear, you look stunning. The navy color really complements your skin tone."

Jordan's magic hazel eyes shift to my face while he politely agrees with my mom. His eyes look green today, with the backdrop of the water behind him. "All the Miller women look lovely tonight," he says diplomatically.

He didn't even give me a direct compliment, but suddenly I'm too warm. I think I'm blushing.

"Can I persuade you to give me one dance, Mrs. Miller?" Jordan turns on his full charm and directs it at my mother.

She nods and takes his arm, allowing him to escort her away. Am I jealous of my own mom right now? As they go, I hear Mom politely mention that Jordan is welcome to stay at their house if he decides to come out to their neck of the woods for my brother's upcoming Idaho game.

He leads her out to the floor, and it's sort of adorable when he takes her hand in his and holds it at shoulder height, with a bent elbow, like they're going to perform a waltz the way I've only seen people do in movies. They sway and box step back and forth to a medium-tempo song I don't recognize.

"You need to go over there and cut in. I can't take how sweet this is. I'm going to need a root canal. Go dance with him. If nothing else, do it for my oral health." Mandy nudges me.

Mads snickers beside her. "Yeah, Shelley. Do it for the *oral benefits*."

Their giggle fit starts back up again.

"Once again, I hate you both very much." But there is no bite in my words when I shake my head and slide away to take a break down near the water.

My sisters like to tease me about the voicemail incident, but they don't know how hard I really am crushing on him now, after our night together. I'm sure they'd encourage it, but I kind of like that I'm starting to build this private connection with Jordan. I'm not ready to put our interactions on display to be analyzed and given the sister treatment.

I want to keep him to myself. He's funny and sweet, and the way he talks to me makes me feel special. He jokes with me, but I can tell he's also trying to be delicate with my feelings in a way other people aren't. I know he sees me as Mikey's little sister, and from his point of view he's probably just being kind, but it still feels like he cares, and that means something to me. Is it a crime if I want to keep that side of our friendship private for now?

I stand at the edge of the pier and wrap my arms around my waist, bracing against the cool breeze as the music up at the tent fades and a new song begins.

Footsteps approach from behind. "Look at this weather acting all mild like it didn't try to kill us four days ago."

The tiny hairs on my arms stand at attention when I recognize the deep voice cutting through the evening air. I turn to see Jordan walk toward me, casually strolling with his hands in his pockets.

I guess talking about the weather is as good a way as any to start a conversation. "Yeah, I heard the storms got really bad down here. Were you all by yourself?"

He nods. "I was. But we only lost power for a few hours at the apartments. It wasn't too much of a hardship. I found ways to occupy myself."

I scan his face for any sign of the smirk I would expect from most guys after that implication, but his expression is neutral. Maybe I'm the one finding innuendo where there isn't any.

"I have a confession. I was worried about you. But I wasn't sure if it would be strange if I checked in. I wanted to, but I also didn't want you to think I was getting clingy after our first conversation."

Jordan sighs as he peers down at his shoes. I think he says, "Nobody checks." Then he clears his throat and shakes his head before looking up again. "Would you hesitate to check on Danielle or Alice if you'd accidentally sent that voicemail to one of them?"

"No, but it's not the same."

"Why not?"

"You know why."

"Do I?"

When his eyes meet mine this time it's too overwhelmingly real. My neck flushes, and my palms begin to sweat. My chest pinches, and I swallow hard to keep myself from saying the words that are too close to escaping. *I want to be the one who checks on you. Because you're different. No one else makes my throat feel tight and my body warm from the inside out like this. And from the way you're looking at me, I think you might even be starting to feel it, too.* But I can't say that, so I stay quiet and chew on the inside of my cheek.

He runs a hand over his face and schools his expression back to neutral. "Shelley, I told you I want to be your friend. You don't have to be afraid to talk to me. I'm not going anywhere."

I nod and swallow again.

"I'm serious," he says.

"I know."

That's what makes things different with Jordan. He takes me seriously.

Standing here next to him, close enough to smell his woodsy cologne, is dangerous. I've been spending so much time chasing an idea of what I want, only for it to walk into my life and stand right in front of me in a tan suit jacket, still just barely out of reach. I want something real. Something honest. It's hard not to see the promise of those things in his eyes. Jordan could be all of that and so much more for some incredibly lucky someone. Just not me. I need to accept that.

Our bodies have been edging closer, and he's only a few inches away when we both turn toward the water to watch the setting sun. The reception will be wrapping up soon. It's windy, and I brush a few strands of hair out of my face as a chill runs through me. This sleeveless dress was perfect earlier in the day, but the temperature is dropping quickly.

"Here. It's getting chilly." He takes off his suit jacket and wraps it around my shoulders. I try not to make it obvious I'm inhaling long whiffs of his scent on the fabric. It smells like cedar, night air, and something uniquely Jordan.

"What are your plans for tonight? Do you want to come back to my place after things wrap up here?" he asks, then quickly adds, "You could invite your sisters."

I'm tempted to take him up on it and not tell Mads and Mandy about the offer, but I know I'll never hear the end of it if they find out I went home with our brother's best man. "I think my family was planning to keep the party going back at the hotel. You could join us there." I smile and he returns one of his own, friendly and disarming.

"Yeah? Maybe I will."

"Good. Hope I see you in a little while, then." I shrug out of the jacket so I can hand it back to him.

He shakes his head. "You keep that. It's cold. I'll get it from you later."

"You sure?"

"Definitely." He takes the coat and gently places it back over my shoulders, and I duck my head to hide my blushing cheeks. I can still feel his eyes on me as I walk back to our table, where my parents are already hugging people goodbye.

Chapter 8

Jordan

It's late when I pull up to the Marnock Hotel, where the Miller family is staying, so I shoot off a quick text asking Shelley if I should still come up.

Me: *I swiped a bottle of sparkling cider and some leftover crab cakes during the clean-up effort. You still awake?*

I wince and run a hand over my beard as I realize the message I just sent looks suspiciously like I'm trying to get into her pants. It's not what I meant, but I may as well have said, "You up?"

Shelley: *Yep. Room 206.*

As I walk down the long hallway toward her room, I wonder again if I should be here. Mike trusts me, and here I am, walking toward his little sister's hotel room after dark like some scumbag.

Shelley and I are just friends. But I know how this looks, and I wouldn't blame anyone who saw me right now in my rumpled dress shirt and suit pants for jumping to the wrong conclusion. Although, she did say her whole family would be here.

The door to her room opens just before I reach it, like she was watching through the peep hole. Shelley leans against the frame, wearing a loose tank top and plaid pajama pants. Her face is pink from scrubbing her makeup away, and her long hair is pulled up into a messy bun on top of her head. She looked pretty at the wedding in that tight, fitted dress, but now she looks peaceful and cozy. I think I like this better. It feels like a window into what it looks like when the mask she wears for the rest of the world is stripped away, and all that's left is what's real. Behind her, I can see my suit jacket hanging on a wall hook.

I hold up the bottle and the take-out container. "I hope you like heartburn and late-night cable."

"Sounds perfect, actually. Come on in. My sisters decided to meet up with some of our cousins down in their room, but I told them I wanted to turn in early. It's been a long day, and I've had enough peopling. I know I promised a party, but it's just me in here. You can join everyone else downstairs, if you want. Or you and I can hang out."

"Seems like that's becoming a regular thing for us." I'm not complaining. "But are you sure you want company? If you're tired, I can go."

"I'm not actually tired. A lot of people and noise at once can be too much for me, but one-on-one is nice."

She holds the door open and steps aside, inviting me into her space. Her suitcase is open on the floor, and discarded clothes are spilling out of it. I step around her belongings and scan the small room. Shelley takes the bottle of cider from me. There are no chairs because the room isn't big enough, and since I'm not about to invite myself into her bed, I stand awkwardly, still holding the foam container filled with mini crab cakes.

"You can sit," Shelley tells me, climbing onto the king-sized bed and patting the space next to her.

She untwists the cap and takes a long swig straight from the bottle in her hand. The carbonation must hit her immediately, because she lets out a loud burp. She looks at me with wide eyes as if she's as surprised as I am by the noise that just came out of her. I have to laugh.

"Oh my god, I'm sorry."

"Is it safe to sit here?" I tease, nudging her slightly as I sit beside her.

"No promises." Shelley offers me the bottle, and I take a sip of my own and set the crab cakes between us. She turns on the TV and flips through the channels until she lands on an old back and white movie. "Have you ever played the lip-reading game?" she asks, popping a miniature crab cake into her mouth.

"I don't think so. What's that?"

She presses the mute button so the movie continues without sound. "I did this all the time with Mandy when we were young. We'd make up something ridiculous they could be saying. Like this." She clears her throat dramatically and puts on an exaggerated transatlantic accent for the female character. "My word! The extraterrestrials have arrived. And their flying saucer landed right in my rose bushes. Do something about this, Clarence!"

"I take it I'm supposed to be Clarence?" There is definitely no actual character named Clarence in this movie. Or any spaceship.

She smiles and nods, motioning for me to take a turn to make something up, so I weave together a long story about how Clarence has been sneaking off every night this week to meet someone in the spaceship.

Shelley snorts. "Wait, are you telling me Clarence is having an interspecies affair with an alien?"

"Nope. I'm telling you Clarence is having an affair with an alien, but it's not interspecies because Clarence is also an alien. Plus, his wife is also secretly an alien. But neither of them knows about the other."

"Okay, plot twist." Shelley laughs. "I see you're a quick learner."

She plucks another crabcake from the box and holds it up to me. I take it and pop it into my mouth. My shoulders shake while she continues to expand the asinine story we've concocted. It's not long until we're cracking up so hard that she snorts again, which causes both of us to laugh even harder.

"Oh my god. It seems like you're getting to hear all of my body's embarrassing noises tonight."

"It doesn't bother me when women make noises," I assure her. I didn't mean for it to sound the way it does, but the air in the room shifts to something thick and meaningful when she turns her face toward mine.

Our eyes stay locked in a silent stand-off until I'm the first one to clear my throat and look back toward the movie. Without looking at her again, I take another crabcake and shove it into my mouth to avoid saying anything else. I can still feel her eyes on me as I chew and swallow, so I turn to face her again.

"I really didn't mean anything by that. And I also wasn't referencing, you know, any of that stuff you shared. I wouldn't tease you about that."

"I didn't think you were. I figured you probably meant sneezing or something. But then my mind went to a different place, and…I kind of wouldn't hate making those noises with someone either."

I blink at her. I have no idea what I'm supposed to say to that, so I go with, "Oh."

The strap on her tank top has fallen off her shoulder, so she pulls it back into place, shifting to tuck her legs to the side. "Not that I think we should do that. I mean, it wasn't an invitation. Unless, you know, you want to. But we probably both have crab breath. Although, it's not like I get that many opportunities, and we're both here. It's just…you know what? Never mind."

"Shelley?" I reach over and put my hand on her knee. Her eyes dart down to where we're now connected, and it seems to calm her down a bit because she takes a breath. "I came over to hang out with you, and that's all I'm planning on doing tonight."

She nods. "Yeah. Totally. I agree. Glad we're on the same page. I was just thinking out loud…"

Her words trail off and I squeeze her leg lightly. I should probably pull away, but I can't seem to stop my hand from resting on her thigh. Shelley glances down, and I pretend not to track the subtle tightening of her jaw and the curve of her neck as she swallows.

We turn our attention back to the movie, but the lighthearted, playful vibe from earlier has given way to a thicker tension. There are words we aren't saying, and they're sucking half the oxygen out of the space. I think she might be getting the wrong idea, and if she is, I need to stop this.

It doesn't matter how much I like her or that hearing her laugh gives me the same adrenaline rush as fielding a line drive. I can't hook up with Mike's sister. He would absolutely shit a brick. I know that. Plus, Shelley is basically a genius. She's looking for more than I can offer. I might be collecting unemployment this time next year. It wouldn't be a good idea for either of us. But, despite all of that, spending the past few days with Shelley is the most fun I've had in a long time, and even knowing I shouldn't be here, I'm not ready for this night to end.

I'm still touching her leg when a noise startles both of us. It sounds like someone is fumbling around trying to get the door open.

"It's probably my sisters," Shelley offers, getting up and walking toward the hall. "Mandy and Mads are staying in the room next door, since that one has two double beds. But I wouldn't put it past them to lose their key cards." She peeps through the hole in the door. "Wait. Honey?"

Shelley opens the door to reveal Danielle's wildcard of a grandma, Honey Daniels. She must've booked her own room at the hotel to give the bride and groom some wedding night privacy at the house she now shares with them.

"Hi," Shelley greets her.

When she looks up and sees Shelley's face next to the room number, Honey says, "Oh. Whoopise. This is 206, not 260. Sorry to bother you, Sugar." She turns to leave, then thinks better of it and faces the room again with a sly, conspiratorial smile. "But while I'm here, you got any protection on you?" She winks and points over her shoulder at the middle-aged man rocking on his heels in the hallway.

He's still wearing his embroidered hotel employee blazer and must be at least twenty years her junior.

Shelley shakes her head. "I'm sorry, but—"

"Oh, I see," Honey interrupts and laughs heartily as she spots me sitting on my bed. "You'll be needing it for yourselves."

"No. We won't. It's just—" Shelley protests but Honey cuts her off again.

"No need to explain. I was never here. C'mon, Martin. Change of plans. Looks like you'll be feasting like a king tonight."

Shelley shuts the door and slowly turns back to the bed, her eyes wide and her eyebrows practically at her hairline.

I let out a deep laugh. "You know what? Good for them."

She nods and joins me on the bed again, seeming only slightly traumatized by the interaction. She runs her fingers over her leg, in the same spot I was touching her a minute ago.

"Sure. But if Honey is my brother's grandmother-in-law, does that make her mine, too? Did my new grandma just ask me if she could borrow a condom?"

I laugh again. "Sort of, maybe. But if it makes you feel any better, she wouldn't have hesitated to ask Danielle and Mike either."

She giggles. We both know that's one hundred percent the honest truth, and also, we will never be telling her brother about how we were sitting in a cloud of sexual tension in a hotel bed on his wedding night when his brand-new grandma came knocking, looking for prophylactics.

I spot something beside her and quickly change the subject. "Uh-oh, what's that?"

She follows my gaze over to her pillow, where the bottom half of a stuffed animal is poking out.

Shelley shoves it further into its hiding spot and out of view. "Nothing. Don't worry about it."

I stretch over her to lift the pillow, catching a whiff of her light floral perfume, and grab the furry bunny. I turn to her friend in my hand. "Does this handsome guy have a name?" I ask, straightening his polka dot bow tie.

She covers her face with her hands, looking mortified and adorable. "Mr. Fluffers," she mumbles into her fingers.

This I absolutely will tease her about. "What was that?" I chuckle, pulling lightly at her wrist.

She sighs and uncovers her mouth to own her truth. "This is Mr. Fluffers. He's sort of an emotional support bunny. I sleep with him at night."

A warm feeling spreads through my chest as she speaks. "And you weren't planning to introduce me to the lucky man who gets to share your bed?"

A small smile finds its way to her face as she pulls Mr. Fluffers from my hand and onto her lap. "Nope."

"Not gonna lie, I'm feeling a little jealous right now."

"Don't worry. I find him rather stuffy." Her smile widens at her terrible joke.

"Oh, did you think I meant I was jealous of him? Nah. I'm jealous that you get to hang out with this suave dude all night." I wink, trying to grab the bunny back, but she wins our tug-of-war and hugs it closer to her chest.

Shelley laughs lightly while my stomach does a somersault.

"Can you believe this guy?" she whispers into the bunny's ear, loud enough for me to hear. "But you know what? I still like him."

I feel my face soften as I look at her, and the moment hangs between us for a beat too long before I say, "Hey, Mr. Fluffers, tell Shelley the feeling's mutual."

Chapter 9

Jordan

Shelley squeezes the rabbit closer to herself as she blinks up at me shyly. "I've been meaning to tell you, thanks for not making a big deal about the voice memo thing. I've been kind of a wreck about it since it happened."

"Like I said, you don't have to be embarrassed about that around me. We don't have to talk about it again. But we can, if you need to."

"That's the problem." She sighs. "I don't want to have to talk about it. I don't even like to think about sex at all. It's not the sex part I don't like, though. It's the thinking. When I do, I get all in my head and I can't stay in the moment. You know, *the* moment. You get what I'm saying, right?"

I pick up the bottle from the nightstand and take a sip of the cider, wishing I had something stronger if we're going to have this conversation now. "Yes, I'm aware how innuendos work. And you're not exactly what I would call a subtle person." That's actually one of my favorite things about her.

"Right. Well, then I get anxious about the fact that I'm not staying in the moment, and I get upset with myself for ruining everything before it ever really gets started."

I nod. "I think a lot of people feel that way. That's kind of how it works for me, too, when I'm with someone. But it takes me a long time to get to that point with a person."

Her eyes flick up to mine, and I realize this is the first time I've mentioned my own hangups to her. Or to anyone.

"You know, it's a little unfair that you know so much about my sex life and I now know more about Honey's love life than I do about yours," Shelley tries to joke, but there's too much truth in it, so neither of us laughs.

I swallow another sip of cider and take a long pause before I ask, "What do you want to know?"

She takes a moment to think before she says, "I feel like since we've spent so much time talking about me, it's only fair for you to have to tell me something personal and embarrassing. First kiss?"

"It was with a girl I dated in high school. Her name was Tiffany. We were together for a while. She was my first for a lot of things, actually, including my first heartbreak."

"Okay, cheater. That's much more endearing than embarrassing."

"You only asked about my first kiss. If I tell you I can still recite every line in the movie *It Takes Two* because it was her favorite, and I watched it every day for a week after she dumped me, will that help?"

Shelley lets out a small laugh and reaches out to squeeze my hand lightly. "A little, but it's also incredibly sweet, so the embarrassment scales of justice are still very unbalanced here."

"What if I told you you're still in my phone as Sea Shell because I saw a photo on social media of you dressed as a mermaid last Halloween?"

"Interesting. But no, that doesn't cut it. We're going to need to break out the big questions, I'm afraid. Like…what kind of porn do you watch? And not to kink shame, but after that last confession, please don't say mermaids."

I shrug. "I don't."

She rolls her eyes at me. Hard. "Come on. You don't want to tell me specifics, that's fine. But you're a single guy in your twenties. Don't expect me to believe you never watch it."

"Do you really want to talk about this?"

"I mean, yeah, I kind of do want to talk about these things. But we don't have to if I'm making you uncomfortable," she assures me.

"It's not that."

"Then what is it?"

"I've seen it," I admit. "Porn just doesn't do anything for me. Yeah, I guess I might be in the minority, but I wouldn't know. It's not like we talk about our porn preferences in the locker room or at poker night. Most people tend to keep those things to themselves." I shoot her a look and raise my eyebrows. The blush that paints her cheeks pink makes me smirk. "My friends and I don't sit around having philosophical conversations about our sexuality, or lack thereof, on a regular basis."

"Believe me, I know. That's why I asked if I could talk to you in the first place. It's not like I can dig deep and figure this stuff out with a guy I just met on an app." She looks down at her hands and starts twirling a hair tie she has around her wrist.

"Is that how you usually find people?"

She snaps the elastic gently against her skin. "I've had my fair share of first dates, but they never go anywhere. Starting law school and making a cross-country move doesn't leave a lot of time for building relationships. Between that and the fact that I've been seeing all these doctors." She heaves a long sigh. "You probably think I'm –"

"No. Whatever you're about to say, I don't," I assure her.

"What did you mean 'lack thereof?'" She steers the conversation back to me.

I shrug again. "Some of us just aren't wired the same way most people are. Or are confused about…things."

"Wait." Shelley sits up straight and faces me fully. "Is this you coming out to me, Jordan?"

Am I? I weigh her question, and Shelley waits, eyes locked on my face, until I speak again.

"Maybe? I honestly don't know. And I know that sounds stupid. It doesn't really feel like an epic announcement. This is exactly what I'm talking about. I don't know how to have this conversation." I blow out a breath and rub both hands over my jaw.

She reaches out and takes one of my hands between both of hers. "You don't have to say anything you don't want to. I'm sorry if I pushed you. I only wanted you to know this friendship goes both ways, and I'm here to listen, too."

"You didn't push. It's not a big deal."

She doesn't argue, but her nose pinches like she doesn't quite believe that, so I try to explain.

"It hardly feels like a coming-out story to announce that I'm only sometimes attracted to people. I know it's not exactly typical, but am I allowed to call myself queer just because I rarely care about sex?"

"Are you asking me or yourself? Because I'm not sure I'm qualified to answer, but I think you get to call yourself whatever you want."

"I mean, yeah. Fair. That's probably what I'd tell someone else, too. But what's the difference between a queer guy who only sometimes likes women and a straight man with a low sex drive?"

"Probably how you feel about the idea of dating outside of that pool. What do you think about dating people who aren't women?"

Once again, my shoulders rise and fall. "I'm more drawn to personalities than physicality. I think I'd be open to it. But you would think if that were going to happen it would have happened by now, right? I was serious about not being attracted to people often. So far, all of my experience has been with women. But maybe that's just because those are the people I've happened to be attracted to."

Shelley's tongue darts briefly out of the corner of her mouth, her nose still scrunched. It still looks like she wants to say something, but she's holding back, trying to be a supportive listener.

"I know," I tell her. It's easy to predict what she wants to say. "Those don't exactly sound like the thoughts of a straight guy, right? But…" I don't know what else to tell her. Or myself.

If this is my ticket into the alphabet community, it feels like cheating. My lack of desire for most humans is not really a hardship. It's not something I'm ever going to be discriminated against for feeling, especially when I'm dating women. I won't be denied a job or a marriage license over it. It won't affect my ability to have kids. At most, some people in my life might rib me a little until I settle down with someone, but I can't see anyone we know acting that way. It hardly feels fair to include myself as a member of the queer community when I can pass for straight so easily. I know other people fight hard to gain access to things I have handed to me. But I also know they put the letters Q and A in LGBTQIA+ for a reason, not to mention the plus sign. I guess I could be the reason?

"All I know is it's pretty rare for me, but I do become attracted to people sometimes, especially after I spend a lot of time with someone and get to know them well."

Like now. The way I keep having to stop my eyes from glancing down her shirt. The way my mouth waters when she raises her arms to fix her ponytail and her flowery scent drifts over to me.

Plus, I do like sex. It's just usually pretty low on my priority list.

"So, you're demi?" Shelley's voice pulls me out of my thoughts. "Sorry if it's insensitive to ask, but I've read about that. It comes up a lot in my research when I'm trying to sort out my own stuff. Not to make it about me."

"You're fine. And to answer your question, I think so. Or something close. I think if I felt that spark more often, I might be pan. But I rarely feel it, so I guess that makes me demi?"

The definition seems to fit. Demisexuality is when you need an emotional connection with someone before you develop a sexual attraction to them. The demi label seems closest to how I feel, but there's so much controversy over whether or not it's dismissive of people who are truly asexual that whenever I try to look it up I end up feeling bad about myself and giving up the search.

"I don't know if I'll ever find exactly the right label, and at this point in my life I don't know if it really matters. So, to answer your original question, I've seen porn, but I'm indifferent to it. It's no different to me than looking at a painting in a museum or looking at my own arm right now. I only see bodies. I don't get turned on by it."

Shelley nods along and squeezes my hand, encouraging me to tell her as much as I want. I've never said any of this out loud to anyone, and it's a little bit terrifying, but also a huge relief to finally be open about this part of myself. I appreciate how she's not talking too much or trying to rush me.

"I knew I was a little bit different when my friends started talking about stealing the lingerie catalogues out of neighborhood mailboxes the day they were delivered. I couldn't understand the appeal. I've never had a physical reaction to a picture or a video of a stranger. But I do know when someone's attractive," I tell her. "I have eyes. I know you're hot, for example. But with most people it's similar to looking at a paint color or a piece of art and thinking 'that looks nice.' My thoughts rarely go beyond that unless I get to know someone really well. When that happens, I get these intense crushes, and I start to catch feelings…hard." I don't want to scare her off, but this isn't something I can control, and it's starting to happen with her.

"So, what I'm hearing is you think I'm hot?" she says, poking my calf with her toe.

"What happened to not making this about you?" I tease, making her laugh.

"Thank you for sharing that with me Jordan. Really. Although, I mean, it might be a *little* about me. We've gotten to know each other pretty well, and apparently you think I'm a total smoke show." She winks as she embellishes. Little does she know, she's not wrong.

"True."

"And I know it's not exactly the same, but if it helps, I feel very similarly about labeling my health issues. I wish I had an answer, but ultimately, I'm not sure getting that answer will change much about my situation anyway. So, I think I might get how you feel, at least a little."

Is it warm in here? A bead of sweat trickles down my spine, and her eyes are fixed on my mouth as I lick my lower lip. I don't think I can lie to myself anymore.

I like this woman. A lot.

But we *can't*. Mike is truly a brother to me, and family is something I don't take lightly. She bites her bottom lip and my body stirs. Shelley Miller is going to be the death of me, if her brother doesn't kill me first.

Chapter 10

Jordan's eyes stay locked with mine while he says, "Your mom was right earlier, you know, that dress looked really good on you tonight."

"But in the neutral, looking-at-paint kind of way, right?" I smile and nudge him.

He returns a smirk of his own as he shakes his head. "No."

His head tilts to the side so slightly it's barely perceptible, but I notice, and I watch as his tongue sneaks out to wet his lips. His focus moves from my eyes to my mouth, then back again.

I'm so confused. It's the universal sign that he wants to kiss me, and I am *definitely* putting out "kiss me" vibes of my own. But he's told me that he never hooks up during the season, and he also *just* said he doesn't feel attracted to people most of the time.

But then he goes and fixes those golden flecks in his eyes right at me while he says things that make my body temperature rise so quickly it feels like I could burn a hole straight through these pajamas, and it makes me think I just might be the exception to every one of his rules.

He drapes an arm over my shoulder. We aren't cuddling, exactly, but his hand stays there, warm and steady, just like his breath. The weight of his touch is comforting, and it isn't long until my own breath slows and becomes even. Something about the calming energy he puts into the room soothes my frayed edges.

Maybe I should go for it? He's probably too loyal to Mike to ever make a move, so I lean in and whisper his name. "Jordan?"

"Hmm?"

"If you don't want me to kiss you, you should tell me now."

He doesn't say anything as I continue to inch my face toward his. I watch his throat bob while he swallows. He's still and silent when my lips brush his, only briefly. He pulls away just a touch and puts his forehead to mine while he moves his hand down to my arm and lightly cups my bicep.

"Shelley?"

"Hmm?" I close my eyes as I repeat the same throaty sound he made a few seconds ago.

Then with two words he invites reality to come crashing back into the room with us.

"We can't."

They're the same words I've been repeating to myself since the first time I met him, but hearing his voice confirm the thought shatters a small piece of me.

"Oh." My face falls and I scoot away, retreating to my side of the bed. "Okay. Sorry. I guess I misread this."

He brushes my apology away with a light shake of his head. "No. You didn't. It's just there's still the long-distance thing, and your brother. I don't want to lead you on. We shouldn't. We *can't.*"

"Right. Yeah. That's fine." My voice is small. We both know it's not fine because all the flirty energy and tense anticipation that were filling the air just a moment ago have dissipated, and my ego is deflating faster than a whoopee cushion run over by a bus.

I know everything he's saying is true. It wouldn't be smart or convenient to start anything with Jordan. I've gone over the excuses hundreds of times. I'm in school. He's committed to the team. Long distance is hard. My brother will murder him. I know all of that. Still.

"But just to be clear, one kiss isn't a contract. I never asked for a relationship." I try to save a little bit of face.

After a few awkward moments of silence, he says, "I should go."

I can't argue because I know Mike would see it that way too, and I don't want to cost them their friendship over my silly crush.

That's all this will ever be. A crush. Maybe even a mutual one. But if Jordan doesn't want it to go any further, I need to find a way to move on, too.

Jordan nods to himself and gives me a quick side hug before scooting out of the bed. He takes his suit coat off the hook where I hung it and drapes it over his arm. Stopping with his hand on the doorknob, he says, "Hey, we're still friends, right? I don't want this to change anything."

"Friends. Yep. Sure. Of course." I swallow and blink away the tears fighting their way to the surface. I won't cry until he's gone. He might not want anything to change, but I wish everything could be different.

"Well, I better…" He doesn't finish his sentence as he opens the door. The words "we can't" hang in the air between us while he shows himself out, leaving me alone in this tiny hotel room with all the memories we just created.

Chapter 11

Jordan

The sun is brutal, sending beads of sweat down my neck and soaking the collar of my jersey. We're up five to three in the fifth inning, but the heat is getting to me, and the top of the Panthers lineup is due up to the plate. Lincoln throws a fastball right down the center, and their hitter makes easy contact. The crack of the bat sends a sharp grounder between second and short. Beauchamp dives a fraction of a second too late, and the ball gets past him. Rodriguez scoops it up and tosses it to second base as the batter rounds my bag. It's a clean hit, but Beau's slower than Mike was, and knowing that my previous shortstop would've fielded that without a problem has me more irritated than is probably healthy.

"Let's pick up the pace out here," I yell before spitting into the dirt, which earns me a glare from Lincoln. The game continues, and we give up two more runs, which ties the score before the inning is over. Normally, I'm a lot more even-tempered on the field, but I hate losing when I know the Carvers are in the stands.

Rodriguez is up first to bat for us, but he pops it up for an easy out. Coach Johnson has me sandwiched in the lineup between Smithy and Beauchamp. Smithy steps toward the batter's box and takes another warm-up swing. As I leave the dugout and head to the on-deck circle, I feel a hand rest on my shoulder.

"You've got this," the rookie tries to encourage me.

I grunt and nod, but it takes everything in me not to turn around and shove the guy. He doesn't deserve it. I know he's trying to be nice, but his presence is so irritating.

It isn't like me to let other people get under my skin like this, but it's been three weeks since the wedding, which means it's been three weeks since I've spoken to Shelley. Even though I know I would make the same choice all over again today because nothing about our situation has changed, I can't stop wishing I had stayed with her in the hotel that night. I should call her. I told her we could be friends, but I can't bring myself to pick up the phone. Without even trying, she's unleashed a cyclone of chaos inside me, and I can't tell which way is up.

Smithy draws a walk and trots to first as I try to shake it off and approach the plate. But my head isn't in the right place, and I swing too early for the first pitch and too late for the second.

"Let's go, Wagner!" I hear the annoying young voice behind me, and I'm distracted as the pitch flies past.

"Strike three!" the umpire booms.

"Damn it." I accept my fate with as much pride as I can muster and walk away, passing the rookie again on my way back. "Do me a favor and keep your mouth shut, would you?" I snap at him. Beauchamp smiles, which only pisses me off more.

"What was that about?" Rodriguez asks as I find my seat next to him.

"Nothing."

"Nothing my ass. You're in a real mood lately."

Beauchamp gets an RBI triple because of course he does. Then another hit sends him home to put us ahead by two more runs. He's beaming when he rejoins us, and the guys reward him with high fives and congratulatory slaps. I force myself to tell him it was a nice hit, but I'm over this.

We manage to keep our lead and pull off the win, which makes Beauchamp the man of the hour in the locker room after the game.

"Nice one, Beau. You really helped us squeak that one out." Lincoln nods.

"Yeah," I echo, hoping it's enough of an effort to keep me from looking like a total jackass. I don't want my sour mood to affect the rest of the team.

"Who wants to celebrate?" Rodriguez asks. "It's karaoke night."

Several of our teammates respond with good-natured groans.

"I'll go, but only if your guitar doesn't," Smithy tells him.

"Miller's in town, and he says he's in," Lincoln adds, looking up from his phone.

Rodriguez pulls me aside, out of earshot from the rest of the guys. "So, are you ever going to tell Miller you're into his sister? Gotta tell you, bro, I thought I was going to have to follow you around that wedding with a napkin to wipe the drool from your face every time you looked at Shelley."

I have to give him credit, the dude is way more observant than you'd think. But I don't want to get into it.

"I don't know what you're talking about, man."

"That's how it's gonna be, huh?"

"That's how it is," I insist, although the look on his face tells me he knows I'm full of shit. "I can't make it tonight anyway. My old coach is in town and we're meeting up for dinner. I need to head over to the restaurant."

Rodriguez cups a hand on my shoulder and nods a quick goodbye. I finish stripping off my uniform and rush through a fast shower. I don't want to keep the Carvers waiting.

At the restaurant, the smell of grease and deep-fried seafood makes my stomach growl as I sit alone at a table, sipping a glass of ice water. When Coach Carver walks into The Blue Crab, he looks the same as usual. A few more grays have made their way to his temples, and his midsection is a little paunchier than when we first met, but I can always count on him to be wearing his typical dark polo shirt tucked into belted khaki shorts. He finishes off the look with white socks hiked up high above his dad sneakers. He holds the door open for his wife, and Ms. Ruth takes her time stepping over the threshold. There's a pale yellow sweater draped over her shoulders and a Tupperware container in her hands.

"Jordan, there's my boy!" His voice booms through the small restaurant as he makes his way to our table.

"Hey, Coach. Thanks for coming." I stand to greet him, and he wraps me in a tight hug.

Coach Carver was the kind of coach who took it upon himself to get involved in his players' lives. When he met me in my first year of high school, he knew Mom and I were struggling. I'm sure it wasn't hard to tell. But he saw how motivated I was and how much I wanted baseball to be my ticket out. So, when he found out I was by myself most nights, Coach and Mrs. Carver started inviting me for dinner a few times a week. By the time I was in my third year on his team, I spent more time at their house than my own.

Coach is the closest thing I've had to a dad for the past fourteen years. He still makes the four-hour drive to North Bay from Baltimore as often as he can to come to a Blue Crabs game or grab lunch with me during the off-season, and once a year he and Ms. Ruth come together for a whole week.

"Wouldn't miss it. Ruthie and I booked four nights over at the Marnock hotel. We're excited for the vacation."

"Sure are." Ms. Ruth smiles as she reaches up to hug me with one arm, holding her Tupperware in the other.

"Is that what I think it is?" I ask, pointing to the square plastic container.

"Of course it is." She smiles and pats my cheek.

Coach Carver shakes his head and says, "Take your damn cookies," but there's humor in his eyes as his wife hands them over.

I open the container and pop one in my mouth right away.

He chuckles as he slides into his seat. "As excited as I am to see you, kid, I might be even more excited to be back at The Blue Crab. I'm starving."

This man will probably be calling me "kid" until I have the same gray hair and beer gut he's sporting now. And I'll happily let him. He picks up a menu and scans it thoroughly. I don't know why he's bothering to look because he orders the same thing every time we're here.

"You getting the seafood club again?" I ask.

"You know it."

When Regina comes over to take our order, Coach Carver asks her for the restaurant's signature sandwich, and I order a crab cake. Ms. Ruth orders the soup. She catches me up on the latest news about their kids and grandkids.

"How was the big wedding?" Coach asks. "The new roommate working out?"

I nod. "So far, so good with Jake. The wedding was actually at his parents' place." I take out my phone to show them a group shot of the wedding party while another picture forms in my brain. I remember Shelley in her dress standing by the water, then later that night back at the hotel in her pajamas.

Frank must notice something in my face because he points at me and asks, "What's that look? Something happen at the wedding you want to share with the class?"

I set my phone on the table. "Not really. It was a nice time."

Ms. Ruth gives me a soft smile as she takes a sip of sweet tea. "I have a feeling there's more to that story."

"Nah," I say, shaking my head.

Coach arches a brow and sets his elbows on the table, one open hand clasped over the other fist, resting his chin on both. They know I'm not telling them something, and I know them well enough to realize they'll get it out of me eventually.

I sigh. "Fine. Maybe there's a girl," I mumble from behind my water glass, taking a big swig so I have somewhere to look besides their faces.

"Oh, yeah?" Coach prompts.

"I mean, she's cool or whatever, but it ends there. She lives all the way in D.C. Plus, her brother is my friend. It's too complicated to start anything."

He shrugs. "Doesn't sound very complicated. D.C. is an easy day trip from here. And in my day, it was a good thing for a guy to know his sister was with someone he could trust."

"I'm not sure Mike would see it that way." I voice my concern and understanding crosses his brow.

Ms. Ruth peers at me thoughtfully. "It's been a long time since I've seen you like this. Whatever is going on between you and this young lady, it looks good on you."

When Regina returns and sets down our food, I thank her and pick up a fork to push my crabcake around the plate. They're right. I haven't felt this way since my only serious girlfriend, and they know how that worked out with Tiffany. She's not here, is she?

I fell hard for my high school sweetheart, but my home life was too unstable. Eventually she decided she couldn't chance falling into the kind of life my family lived. I still remember what Tiffany said the day she dumped me. *You're a nice guy, Jordan. You really are. But I need someone with a brighter future.* It gutted me, but even then, I understood. The evidence was on her side. Now here I am, a full decade later, and my future's still a crapshoot.

Shelley is smart and she's driven. She's going to be a lawyer. I, on the other hand, barely managed to get through high school and I'm probably going to be out of a job in a few months. Even if she has feelings for me, I'm sure they'll fade fast as soon as she realizes I've got nothing to offer. That's the way this goes.

My phone lights up with a new notification.

Shelley: *Just had the Worst. Date. Ever. Not exaggerating. Worst one in the history of the world. God awful.*

I'm hit with a queasy feeling that has nothing to do with the crab cake.

Shelley's dating?

Then again, why wouldn't she be? I told her outright nothing would ever happen between us and catapulted myself into the friend zone the first time she tried to touch me.

I hate this. And I did it to myself. I can't blame anyone but me.

My face must do something stupid again while I stare at her message because Frank chuckles and points down at my screen. "You need to take that?"

"No, I'll talk to her later."

He nods. "I hope you do."

The rest of the meal is pleasant, and it's always great to spend time with the Carvers, but a small part of me is still worrying about Shelley. She's obviously fine. If it were anything serious, she'd call her family or even the police. Not me. I'm sure she only wants to vent. But knowing she's upset at all doesn't sit right with me, and I have a hard time forcing down my food. Exactly how bad was this date?

At the end of our meal, Frank tries to pay, like he always does, and he's put-out to learn I was a step ahead of him and cleared the bill with Regina before they got here. I'm grateful to be in a place where I can finally be the one treating them to a meal and at least pay back a tiny bit of their generosity.

As we stand to go, I thank them for visiting, and Ms. Ruth rests a hand on my arm. "We wouldn't miss it. We look forward to this trip all year. Watching you play has always been such a treat for us. We're proud of you, Jordan."

I clear my throat and nod at her, not quite sure what to say. Her words are kind, but my gut sinks. Baseball is what connects me to the Carvers. When I'm no longer playing, how often will I see them?

She squeezes lightly. "Well, we better get back to our room. I need a nap after all the excitement of that game of yours. And you have a phone call to make." She reaches out, and when I bend down to hug her, she whispers, "You deserve to be happy, Jordan. If this young lady can bring some more joy into your life, let her. Don't talk yourself out of it. You do that sometimes, you know."

I wave as they leave, then I head home, willing myself not to call Shelley too soon after getting her text. I don't want to look desperate, but I need to hear her voice.

Chapter 12

Jordan

"Hey, man. Long time no see," Jake says as soon as I step into the apartment. He grabs a bottle of soda out of the fridge and pulls a jar of peanuts down from a cabinet.

I drop my bag and collapse onto the couch. "Yeah, we had a long stretch this week."

"How'd everything go?" Our games aren't usually televised, so he wouldn't know. He's in the stands on occasion, but for the most part my new roommate is the quiet, artistic type. He spends most of his days in his new community studio, which has made the transition to living together incredibly easy. We're rarely home at the same time.

"We're in the middle of a series against the Panthers," I tell him. "So far, we've won two, lost one. Three more to go." After years of living with Mike, I'm not used to having to update someone else. It's kind of nice because I know Jake's only being polite, and I never have to talk shop with him if I don't want to. I can leave things on the field, like the details about striking out today.

Jake nods and sinks down onto the other side of the sofa. He looks even more exhausted than I feel. He and Alice invested in a building over on Main Street and Jake's remodeling it himself. The manual labor has him drained.

"Want to watch something?" He grabs the remote and points it at the TV, turning on Weekly Wrap-Up, the satire news show. His head falls to his chest and he's asleep before the first segment ends.

I turn the volume down a few notches and try not to laugh too loudly while I continue watching. A few minutes later, my phone vibrates in my pocket.

Shelley: *Seriously. Why are men?*

I give in, finally typing out a reply.

Me: *Why are we what?*

Shelley: *Uggggh. Just…why?*

Me: *All right. What happened?*

Shelley: *Once upon a time, some bozo invented the internet, then along came online dating, and here we are. So, back to my original question. Why? Are? Men?*

Me: *I take it this is about the date that did not go well?*

Shelley: *If by well you mean he showed up forty minutes late and got a nosebleed during our meal, which he tried to clean with the tablecloth, then it was great.*

Shelley: *Oh, and he also conveniently forgot his wallet, so I had to pay for the meal he ordered for himself AND the one he ordered for his mommy (which is what he still actually calls her, by the way).*

Me: *Yikes.*

Shelley: *Then my first rideshare cancelled, so I had to wait a half hour in the dark for another car to show up.*

Me: *Ok, yeah. That's pretty bad.*

Shelley: *I swear, I just want one good date. Just one. Is that really so much to ask?*

Me: *I'd like to say no, but the evidence is not on my side.*

Shelley: *Jordaaaan!*

I laugh because I can almost hear her pouty whine through the phone screen. Jake stirs, so I take my phone into my room, grabbing an ice pack from the freezer on my way, to continue this conversation with more privacy.

Shelley: *It's me, isn't it? I'm the common denominator in all these situations. Tell me what I'm doing wrong. I can take it. (Probably.)*

Me: *No way. Not falling into that trap. Maybe reframe and be glad you dodged a bullet?*

Shelley: *A bullet would at least make me feel something.*

Time to switch this to a face-to-face conversation. I press the video call icon next to her name. She picks up, looking surprised.

"Talking about bullets earns you a courtesy check," I tell her.

She smiles and rolls her eyes as she props her phone up on a piece of furniture, changing the angle. "Completely unnecessary, and also I'd like to point out you're the one who brought up the bullet, but the well-check is appreciated nonetheless."

"Just had to see for myself."

"Well, here I am." She waves a hand up and down her body, and my eyes scan to follow it. It's obvious she put a lot of effort into getting ready for this date. Her hair is hanging down her shoulders in loose curls, and a tight, long-sleeved red dress hugs her curves. She's wearing a little bit of eye makeup, but the rest of her face looks natural.

Even though I can't smell her, I remember her light floral scent from the hotel room. My body stirs to attention at the memory.

"You should go back out and take yourself on the kind of date you want. You look great. Don't waste all that effort on some loser. Do it for you."

She sighs. "I know you're right, and I appreciate the sentiment, but it's late and I'm tired. Plus, I think I would just feel pathetic and lonely knowing I'm only out on my own because I got rejected *again*."

The implication that I was the last person who made her feel this way stings, but we both know there were legitimate reasons for that. It's baffling how anyone else could ever walk away from her.

"Take me with you, then." The words are out of my mouth before I have a chance to think about them. When she scrunches her brow, I clarify, "I'll stay on the phone. You won't be alone."

"Surely, you have something better to do tonight than babysit me."

I really don't. "Sadly, no. Just icing my elbow. And I was planning to binge some old sitcom reruns. This will be way more entertaining." She narrows her eyes at me, but I push a little more because I get the sense she needs it. "Go on. You know you want to."

She rolls her bottom lip between her teeth as she considers. "Honestly? I'd rather just get out of this dress. Shapewear is not for the weak. Excuse me a second."

She repositions the phone to face the opposite wall as she walks toward her closet, which I can see in the reflection of the mirror hanging on the wall her phone is now facing. I cough to try to get her attention, but she's too far away to hear me.

I try not to watch as Shelley peels off her dress, revealing a matching black lace bra and panty set, along with some tight contraption around her middle, which does look really uncomfortable. It's fastened with about a dozen tiny hooks, and it takes her a few minutes to twist it around and unhook them all. She moans in relief as it falls away, and even though I don't have a full view of her front, I strongly consider moving the ice from my elbow down to my lap.

When she reaches behind her back to unhook her bra, I speak up again. "I can see you, Shelley."

Her eyes meet mine in the mirror, and she bites the corner of her smile. If she didn't already know, she does now, and she's teasing me on purpose. Little brat. I put my hand over my eyes, peeking only a little as she slides on a silky tank top. Then she pulls on a pair of pastel sleep shorts covered in rubber ducks. She walks toward her phone and my eyes lock on the two hard peaks visible through the fabric of her shirt until her face is in full view again.

"Do you want to walk me through what else happened on this date?" I ask, pushing through the lump in my throat and trying to be here for my *friend*.

"Um, okay. If you think that will help. But I'm telling you, it was a disaster."

"I'm sure it wasn't all bad. Start at the beginning."

"We met at the restaurant, and it was your typical second date. I'd met him for coffee once before. There was small talk, I tried to start up a little bit of banter, but he didn't really seem to get my jokes."

I ignore the pang of discomfort I feel at the thought of this idiot getting a second date from her. "What kind of jokes were you making?"

"Good ones, obviously."

"Like what? I'm trying to figure out if he's as dumb as I think he is."

She huffs. "Fine. It was a seafood restaurant. There was one point where the server asked if we'd like to order mussels. I said if I knew it was that easy to get them, I would stop wasting so much time at the gym."

"Ouch. There's no excuse for the bleeding on tableware or the mommy issues, but that one's a little bit on you. That's an objectively terrible joke."

"Was not. The server laughed."

"Yeah, because it's their job to put up with stuff like that."

She groans. "I thought you were supposed to be helping. You told me I could talk to you about these things."

"Sorry. Go on. Then what happened?"

"Not much. It was lame. He hardly spoke to me. Before the nosebleed fiasco, he took four calls on speakerphone at the table: his mom twice, his banker, and another woman he's apparently seeing tomorrow night. We ate some, then he bled everywhere and said he needed to get back to his apartment to let his dog out. He asked if I wanted to swing by later and meet the dog."

Why is she wasting her time getting upset about this dickhead? "Was there really a dog, or is that a euphemism?"

Shelley lets out a pained sound. "Ew. I hadn't considered that possibility until this moment, so thanks for that. I assumed there was an actual dog, but now that you mention it, he never said the dog's name or what breed it was. But it doesn't matter because I said no thanks and told him I have an early class."

"Do you?"

"Not really. I needed an out. My first class is at ten." An unexpected flood of relief hits me as she says it.

"So, what's this call really about, then?" If she didn't like the guy, I'm not sure what she wants me to say here. I'm not going to help her orchestrate hookups with people she doesn't even like.

A low groan comes back at me. "I hate that you're making me say it. I guess I'm just lonely and…frustrated."

"Frustrated how?"

"Come on, Jordan. Don't act dense. I know things got a little intense at the hotel, but I don't have anyone else to talk to about this stuff. You said I could ask for your help with this."

"What I said was if you ask me questions, I'll do my best to answer them. So far, I haven't heard a single question out of you." There's a pause, which I take as her admission she knows I'm right. I hate this guy for making her second-guess herself, and it sucks that he wasted her time tonight, but I know I have no right to be jealous here. I'm the one who pumped the brakes at the hotel.

"Technically, I did ask a question. I asked, 'Why are men?'" she insists. Then her voice comes out small and quiet when she asks what she really wants to know. "Do you think…do you think I'm broken?"

My chest squeezes. I don't even bother trying to school the pained expression on my face, but I try to keep my own voice neutral and not sound as sad and exasperated as I feel when I say, "No. I don't."

"Maybe I'll just never be able to connect with someone the way other people can. And as much as I'd like to be okay with it and take pleasure in my own company, it turns out I can't even do that right. My body is defective."

I want to tell her that between my elbow issues and my own confusion, I know the feeling two-fold, but I don't want to pull focus onto myself. She reached out because she needs a friend. Right now is supposed to be about her.

I sigh and scrub a hand over my face. "I won't make any comments about that, other than seeing as how you've already been to multiple doctors, we know it's not a problem with your anatomy. I doubt this is going to last forever. You said they told you it was a mental block, right?" Honestly, as much as I relate, it's getting a little tiresome to have to keep repeating myself about this. Shelley is so sure of herself in every other aspect of her life, it's hard to watch her fumble over her own insecurities when it comes to her body. But I know I can't make a habit of telling my best friend's sister how hot I think she is. "It's okay to be alone, you know. Maybe take dating off the table for a while. Or just take some time to figure out what you actually want."

Shelley's face falls. I must've said something wrong, but I can't think what. I was trying to be careful.

"Okay. This was maybe not such a great idea after all. I'm gonna go." She hangs up before I can say goodbye.

I shake my head and stare at the phone in my hand for a solid minute before a light tap on my doorframe causes me to look up and see Jake rap on it with his knuckles.

"I shouldn't have taken that nap. Now I can't sleep. Do you want to play a few rounds of Mario Kart or something?" His head tilts, noticing the expression on my face. "You good?"

Am I good? I have no valid reason not to be. Shelley's giving me the space I told her I wanted. But there's a dull headache brewing in my left temple anyway. "Sure. I'll be there in a minute."

Looking down at my phone again, I wonder if I should try to say something encouraging to her. I don't like the way we keep ending things, but I also don't want to make a big deal out of something that shouldn't be. I toss my phone onto my bed and walk out of the room, shutting the door on it for now.

Chapter 13

Shelley

I slam my book shut and give up pretending to concentrate on studying. Every spare brain cell I have is still dedicated to dissecting last night's conversation. Maybe it was rude to hang up on Jordan, but I *do* know what I want. I'm just not ready to hear him tell me once again why I can't have him. Or apparently why I shouldn't be with anyone else either. Or maybe I'm being harsh, because he didn't actually say that.

Sor—I only type half of an apology text before I think better of it and delete the message.

You know what? No.

I'm not apologizing. He's the one out here sending all these mixed signals. He doesn't get to reject the idea of being with me, say we can only be friends, and then act put out when I try to be friends with him. *Like he asked for.* What exactly does he want me to do? Not date him, but also ignore all other men for the rest of my life? Screw that. I'm a grown-ass woman with needs.

Then again, maybe I'm being unfair. Should I stop talking to him about this stuff? I know I should probably cool it with the flirting.

The strip tease was a bit much, I'll admit. But if we're really supposed to be friends, Jordan could at least also make an effort. Before yesterday, I hadn't heard from him in weeks. And I had to be the first one to reach out.

At the hotel, it seemed like he enjoyed talking to me. I thought we were confiding in each other. I really like being able to get Jordan's perspective. His advice helps me get out of my own head and look at things a little more objectively. But maybe I still really am just Mike's little sister to him. Maybe I don't mean as much to him as he means to me.

Okay, apparently talking to him doesn't *always* get me out of my head, considering my current thought patterns are pretty much the definition of overthinking.

Whatever.

I don't have time for this. I pull out my laptop and click the link in my email for my telehealth appointment with my psychiatrist. It takes a few minutes beyond my scheduled appointment time, so I'm bouncing my knees and picking an eraser apart, shredding it into piles of red dust by the time Dr. Rappon pops onto the screen.

"Hi, Michelle. How's everything going?"

"Um, fine, I guess?"

"School is good? And your family?"

"Yeah. Family is great. My brother got married recently, and we all had a nice time at the wedding. School is going well." It's always been easy for me to memorize facts and dates, so learning about statutes and regulations comes naturally. It's the social aspect that can be hard for me. That, and managing my time and staying organized. But my grades are fine.

"Glad to hear it. So, how can I help you today?"

"I was hoping to talk about my meds."

He nods. "Of course. That's why I'm here."

I swallow. "Um, I also had bloodwork done recently, so I wanted to make sure you saw that, too, in case you need it."

"Let me pull up your chart. Yep. It's right here. Everything looks good to me. All your levels are within a normal range."

"Cool. So, I do have a question..."

He waits a few seconds, but when I still don't ask, he prompts, "Yes?"

"Sorry. It's just, I was wondering, could this medicine have any, uh, side effects...of the sexual variety?" I look down at my hands, brushing away some of the eraser crumbs, and pick at my thumbnail.

He responds gently. "Every medication comes with several side effects. Is there something specific you're experiencing?"

I take a breath, reminding myself he's a doctor as I look up into the screen again. "It's actually more like *not* experiencing." I feel my face redden. Why does my psychiatrist have to be so young and so *male*? Would it be too much to ask to get these conversations translated through cartoon avatars or something?

"I see. Well, yes. Unfortunately, while meds can be very helpful in some areas, the improvements they make to our lives do come at a cost. As far as this medication goes, it wouldn't be unusual for a patient to experience things like decreased libido, personal dryness, or anorgasmia. On the opposite end of the spectrum, some folks report a noticeable increase in those areas. It just depends on your body's unique chemistry."

"What's anorgasmia?"

"The inability to achieve a climax during intercourse."

Right. I should've figured that out from the context clues. Now I feel dumb. Of course there's an actual medical term for not being able to come. "And that's a side effect of this particular ADHD medicine? My gynecologist said it might be worth looking into. Oh, and she also prescribed me a cream with estrogen in it. That won't cause any interactions with my other medicines, will it? I think it might be helping a little."

"I don't think the cream will cause any negative reactions. Glad to hear you think it's doing its job. Obviously, if it causes a rash or burning, then stop using it because you might be allergic. Otherwise, it might actually improve the efficacy of your stimulant."

"Really?"

He nods again. "There are theories and anecdotal evidence that increasing estrogen levels could have a positive effect on dopamine levels and executive functioning skills during menopause as well as in women with ADHD."

"Only anecdotal evidence?"

"Unfortunately, we still have a lot of work to do when it comes to understanding women's bodies," he says, diplomatically.

It's good to know Jo is out there trying to do the research.

Dr. Rappon continues, "As far as the anorgasmia being related to the stimulant, yes. It's possible. These medications affect neurotransmitters in the brain, and occasionally that can lead to difficulties in the way our bodies function in other areas."

Even though intellectually I knew I wasn't doing anything wrong, I'm still hit with an immediate wave of relief hearing him confirm there could actually be a legitimate medical reason for my problem. And it's not just me. Although, it sucks to be part of the decreased libido group and not the fun one. Figures.

"Would, um, would anorgasmia be a good enough reason to try a different medication?"

Dr. Rappon gives me a level look. "My job is to help you find what works best for you. If you aren't satisfied with your current meds for any reason, we can either adjust the dosage or try something else."

"I'm definitely not satisfied," I admit with a smirk, letting a little humor come through.

A small smile crosses his face as he picks up on my double-meaning. "No problem. I'd prefer to wean you off one drug slowly before we try another. How about we try this: I'll write this month's prescription for a lower dose, and we'll see how you feel, especially adding the estrogen. If you find you're still experiencing these symptoms by our next appointment, we'll talk about some other options. Sound good?"

"Yes. Thank you."

With my medication plan settled, at least I know I can head to class this afternoon with a clear conscience and a loose semblance of a plan. I've got this. Maybe I don't even need Jordan after all.

I'd still like to talk to someone about my body who truly understands, so I finally reach out to Jo. Only this time, I'm not taking any chances sharing this information with her over the phone, so I shoot off a quick text to ask if she can meet in person.

Me: *Hey! I know it's been a while. I've been following your posts, and I love seeing you absolutely kill it professionally. I'll be coming home soon for a quick visit. Think you'll have time to grab lunch and catch up?*

She writes back quickly.

Jo: *Absolutely! I'd love to see you. Let me know where and when. I'll be there.*

Through a few more brief texts, we make plans to meet at our favorite cafe the day after Mike's game.

Jo: *Can't wait! See you soon.*

Chapter 14

Jordan

Punching a fist into my glove, I get set as Beauchamp steps up to the plate. Coach Johnson has divided us into two teams for practice. Beauchamp is one of the opposing team's best hitters, and he's already scored on us twice in this scrimmage.

The Blue Crabs had a rough season last year, but lately we've been on a winning streak, and I'm not going to be the reason it ends, if I can help it. So, I'm putting my all into this practice.

Beau makes contact on the first pitch and sends a line drive straight over my head. I jump up, stretching to snag the ball out of the air. When I make the catch, Beau stops short and turns to head back to the dugout.

I shake out my elbow and smile, knowing I do still have at least *some* life left in my game. But I don't know how much longer I want to do this. Is it even worth it anymore?

This isn't as easy as it used to be. Twenty-eight isn't old, but it's the oldest I've ever been, and I'm feeling every single day of it. As much as I love the game, this is the only body I'm going to get, and the thought of destroying it to stretch out my career for another season or two is starting to seem kind of stupid.

I know I need to talk to Coach Johnson, but I'm dreading the whole conversation. Not to mention, I have no plan. What am I supposed to do with myself after I quit? Technically, there's nothing tying me to North Bay. I could go anywhere, do anything. Or maybe not *anything*. But anything a mostly able-bodied twenty-something without a degree or any formal job training can do. Which doesn't leave a lot of options, especially in a small town. But I like it here. It's the first place I've been able to settle down and feel like I'm building a life.

As we wrap up and head to the locker room, Rodriguez jogs up next to me. "You better be there tonight. I'm not taking no for an answer this time. You've missed the last three poker nights. The Foxhounds have a late game. We'll keep the TV on and watch Mike play."

"Yeah, I'm coming," I assure him.

"Good. Davis will be there, too. And feel free to bring Jake."

"I'll ask him," I promise. "You sticking around for conditioning?"

"Nah. I'm gonna head out and set up."

As he leaves, I make my way down to the weight room.

Shelley is living in my head rent-free, and I need to get her out of there for the sake of my sanity. I figure optional conditioning is as good as any other place to try to clear my thoughts. But my efforts are in vain, because the last conversation we had is still playing on a loop in my mind as I finish with the leg press and move to the weight bench.

I'm sure I could've handled it better when she tried to talk to me, but I don't know how.

And if I'm being honest, this funk I'm in isn't only about her.

I rack the weights and sit on the bench, running a towel over my face. I lift my chin at Robin, who's been keeping an eye on my set from across the room, probably worried I'm going to counteract all the hard work she's been doing on my elbow.

She comes toward me. "Everything cool with you, Jordan? Seems like you're deep in your own head again today."

I nod, tossing the towel into the laundry basket against the wall. "Yeah. Sure. I'm fine."

She puts her hands on her hips and purses her lips, making her patented *Do you expect me to believe that?* face. I guess if there's someone here who might be able to relate to at least part of my dilemma, it's Robin.

Scanning the room to make sure no one is paying attention to us, I lower my voice. "Can I ask you something personal?"

"You can ask. Doesn't guarantee I'll answer. But go ahead."

I'm not sure how to approach this, but I guess the best way is to take a breath and say it. "Have you always known you're into women?"

She runs her tongue over her teeth and takes a second before responding cautiously. "Yes. Why do you ask?"

I close my eyes and try to lean into the truth. "Because I'm almost thirty, and my own preferences are still not something I have a solid grasp of. I never spent a lot of time thinking about it before, if I'm being honest. I just went with whatever felt right at the time. But lately it's on my mind a lot, and me not understanding myself is starting to affect other people. Maybe that sounds ridiculous." I shrug.

"It doesn't," Robin assures me, shaking her head. "As far as the age thing, there's no correct timeline for when people can decide to embrace their identity. Maybe you're just growing up?"

"There's this girl," I admit.

"Woman, I should hope," Robin corrects, and I nod.

"Yes. There's a woman. I like her. A lot. And we've been talking about, well, everything. Except when I tried to tell her about this, I'm not sure I explained it well."

"What did you say to her?"

"That I think I'm probably demi. She understood that. But I've never thought I needed to give it a label, you know? And now… there are still a lot of questions even I don't know how to answer."

"Is she pressuring you to label yourself?"

"Not at all. But we did have a long talk about it. Now I feel almost, I don't know, disingenuous, maybe? I know I'm giving her a lot of mixed messages. She ended our last conversation kind of abruptly." I keep blaming my friendship with her brother, and it's true that I don't think Mike would be thrilled at the thought of me hooking up with his sister. But it's also not fair to any of us that I'm using him as an excuse to push Shelley away.

I roll my head back, staring up at the ceiling. "I know I'm holding back because I don't actually know who I am or what I should do. The demi label does fit the best, I guess, but nothing I've read about any label feels like it fits me one hundred percent, so how should I know?"

I totally understand why Shelley has been going to doctors and looking for answers about her body. Not having them can drive a person crazy. When I pause, Robin stays quiet until I go on. "Yet, I'm the only one who *can* know. And I can tell myself it doesn't matter, but it does. If I don't even have the language to explain how my own mind and body work, then how am I ever supposed to build something worth having with another person? I don't know if I have it in me to be a good partner. I've never had a serious adult relationship. And that's incredibly depressing. Does that make sense?"

Robin lets out a slow breath and sits down next to me on the narrow weight bench, both of us looking straight ahead, into the mirror on the wall. "Wow. You really did have a lot on your mind, huh?"

"Yep."

"And you really like her, don't you?"

I sigh. "Yeah. I really do. But…" I turn up my palms and shake my head, unsure where to go from here.

Our eyes connect in the mirror, and Robin's track pants make a swishing sound as she scoots closer to wrap an arm around my back. "It makes plenty of sense, Jordan. I can't answer those questions for you, but I can tell you this: You aren't alone, and you're right on time. I'm here anytime you want to talk about it, but you're right. You're the only person who can figure out what works for you. And it might take a while before you find the words that fit. But can I tell you something else?"

"Please."

"It can be a lot of fun making those discoveries with someone else." Robin winks into the mirror, and it makes me chuckle and lightens the mood. She nudges me. "It sounds like you've found someone you feel comfortable with who wants to know you on a deeper level. In my book, that's a good thing. Romantically or not, at the end of the day, isn't that what we're all looking for? Maybe younger Jordan wasn't wrong. It's okay to do what feels right here."

I nod. "Thanks, Rob. I needed to hear that."

"Anytime. I can also promise you that any person on this team can vouch for the fact that you're an excellent teammate. You have nothing to worry about there. If you decide you want a relationship with this woman, then I'm pretty confident you're going to do everything humanly possible to rock her world." That makes me smile. "Finish up and go get some rest. But I want more ice on that elbow as soon as you're done in here, yeah?"

"Yes, ma'am."

She stands and gives my shoulder a squeeze before taking off. I hit the shower for a quick rinse and head out for poker night, feeling a little bit lighter.

Chapter 15

Jordan

Davis looks at me over the table, then back down at his cards before folding. "This might be my last hand," he says, rubbing a palm over his eyes. Poor guy is exhausted. "I still have billing paperwork to finish tonight, and I wanted to return some emails before it gets too late."

Once or twice a month we sit around at Rodriguez's place and play cards with a few guys on the current team, and sometimes—like tonight—an old teammate will drop in. Clark Davis was the Blue Crabs' shortstop before Mike. There's been a ton of turnover in that position. Now Davis runs a hauling business that's taking off faster than anyone could have expected. Who knew so many people were willing to pay someone else to clean out their old junk?

"Sounds like it's going well," I offer, adjusting the ice pack on my arm. "You must be bringing in a lot of clients if you have all that to do."

"It is, but I think I need to bring on some staff. It's getting to be too much for me to handle on my own. I hired a few teenagers to help get that busted-up fridge out of Edna's kitchen last week, but it's getting to the point where I need to consider more permanent help."

"I can confirm, bringing in a partner for the art studio was the best decision I've ever made," Jake says, laying his cards face down on the table. "I fold."

"Yeah? I raise." I push a short stack of red chips toward the center of the table.

Davis nods. "Yeah, maybe I should look for some help."

"I call," Rodriguez says, sliding his chips into the pot.

We show our cards, and his three kings beat my two pair. While Rodriguez collects his winnings, we turn our attention to the TV. The Foxhounds game is starting, so we take a break to watch our buddy's new team play the Orioles for a bit.

There's an uncomfortable feeling in my chest when Mike's face briefly flashes across the screen. I'm proud of my friend, but it also sucks to know it will never be my face up there. Mostly, though, it stings to know I'm thinking about walking away from the game that saved me. When my relationship with my mom started to crumble and Coach Carver stepped up, baseball gave me a lifeline. The game's been the best friend I ever had. And someday soon I'm going to turn my back on it.

Davis gets up to leave, and I nod toward the balcony. "Before you go, can we step out for a minute?"

"Sure," he answers me, cautiously. His forehead creases, but he nods and follows me outside. "Everything okay?"

I sigh and scratch at my beard, looking back through the sliding glass doors, where I can see my teammates taking turns tossing cheese puffs in the air and trying to catch them in their mouths.

"Actually, never mind. Maybe I shouldn't do this here. We can have this conversation another time."

He looks concerned. "Nah. Now you've got me curious. Talk to me, man."

"I guess I have two main things I wanted to ask." I tug at a loose piece of thread on the hem of my shirt. Maybe I should've prepared for this. It feels awkward to wing it.

"Shoot."

"The first one is how did you know you were ready for retirement?"

He blinks. "Wow. Okay. Not where I thought this was going. I thought you were going to tell me you were short on cash and ask me to spot you for the next round. Or maybe tell me you needed me to look at a rash or something. I really thought we were about to play *is this jock itch or an STI?*"

"Why the hell would I come to you for that?"

"You'd be surprised how many guys ask. But it seems like the kind of thing you'd go to Miller with, seeing how tight you two have always been. Plus, with your whole celibacy thing, I'm surprised. I mean, how did you even get it?" Davis eyes my crotch suspiciously.

"I didn't! There's no rash! You made it up." I throw my hands up, exasperated.

Rodriguez misses the cheese puff he's going for and glances in our direction as he searches for his lost snack.

Not wanting to bring any more attention to myself, I tone my voice down and repeat, "I don't have a rash."

"If you say so. Why are you asking about retirement? Does this mean you're thinking about hanging it up?"

I shrug, then give a small nod. "I think I have to. It's the elbow. I'm not bouncing back the way I used to."

With a sigh, he cups my shoulder. "I get it. There comes a point when you just know. For me, it was when I realized the whole team played better when Miller was on the field and I took a seat on the bench."

"It's the same for me this season," I admit. "I've been working with Robin for a year, and it's not improving. And I'm struggling to keep up with the younger guys. Beauchamp is running circles around me."

He gives me a sympathetic look. I know he knows how it feels. "What's the second thing?"

I smooth a hand through my hair. "Uh, do you have any job openings?" Davis laughs, and my stomach sinks, but I'm quick to try to sell myself. "I mean, I know I don't have a lot of experience in the hauling business, but I feel like I could pick it up pretty quickly. I'd like to stay in North Bay, and you know how limited the job market is here."

He holds up a hand. "Dude. Stop. Of course I have a job for you, whenever you want one. But the idea of being your boss is a little bizarre."

Now it's my turn to laugh. "Fair."

"I've gotta tell you, though, if you're leaving the game because the physical stuff is too hard, getting into the moving business isn't going to help. It won't be any easier on that elbow." He makes a good point. "I could try you in the office after this season wraps. How are you with computers? Wanna learn bookkeeping?"

I nod, grateful for the offer. "Thanks, man. That might work. I'm up for anything."

"Cool. I'll be in touch. And make sure to get that rash checked out," he kids and punches me lightly on the arm.

I roll my eyes as he leaves, but after talking with Robin earlier and now knowing I could have a job lined up, the heaviness I've been feeling is starting to lighten up a little.

Chapter 16

Shelley

I stand motionless in front of the communal mailboxes, staring at the pink paper in my hand. The one I found crumpled and stuffed into the back of the slot for my apartment. It's a letter from the housing department, dated two weeks ago. Apparently, I've been forgetting to check my mail for a while.

My eyes scan over the words again, as if they will have magically changed sometime within the last thirty seconds. Unfortunately, even upon further inspection, it's still the same letter I read the first, second, and third times.

Dear Graduate Residents,

As per the email sent on the eighth of April, our graduate housing will be closed for the summer months so that the buildings can be mitigated for mold and inspected for any further water and structural damages caused by last month's storm. Graduate apartments will reopen the last week of August. Room and board fees will not be charged for the dates the space remains unavailable. We apologize for any inconvenience and look forward to seeing everyone upon the start of the fall semester. Thank you.

Dean Winters

The thunderstorms did get nasty in our area, but who knew the tropical storm that passed through caused so much damage on campus? Why didn't anyone mention this in class? I know a lot of people leave campus over the summer, but I can't possibly be the only one who was planning to stay.

I don't remember seeing a message, but sure enough, when I open my email on my phone, there it is, mocking me. I'm sure they probably called about this, too, but I usually delete the robocalls from the school without bothering to listen because the fundraising requests and parking issues don't apply to me.

Welp.

This is a disaster.

I was hoping to get a summer job or an internship, but now missing out on those opportunities is the least of my worries. I need a place to live.

Since I won't be charged for my apartment, I'll still have the money from my student loans, but that was meant to cover cheap student housing. I don't know if I can afford to stay, or even find something available, anywhere else in this city over the summer.

Think, Shelley.

But no good options spring to mind.

Going all the way back to Idaho doesn't make much sense when I have other family nearby. I think I need to swallow my pride and call my brother. I wince at the thought of having to beg to move in with him.

Before I start to hyperventilate, I pull out my phone. He's going to love this, though. If there's one thing my brother does better than anyone else I know, it's play the hero. He lives for solving other people's problems. This time I'm going to have to let him.

How did I let myself get into this situation?

Mike answers on the third ring. "Hey, Shelley, what's up? You're on speaker. I'm in the car with Danielle and Alice."

There's no point in dragging this out with pleasantries, so I jump right to the reason for my call. "How would you all feel about taking in a displaced law student for the summer? Namely, me. Your sister. Who you love and respect and would not want to see left unhoused in a big city for two months while her school rewires the building and repairs a bunch of mold or whatever other storm damage they're talking about in the notice I've been given."

Danielle screeches. "Ew, have you been living with mold?! Of course you can stay with us. It might get a little tight adding another roomie, but we'll manage. But please know, I take no responsibility whatsoever for Honey's actions during your stay."

I laugh, remembering Honey's late-night visit to my hotel room. "Understood."

Mike's tone is also concerned. "What about your classes?"

"I won't be able to take any this summer, I guess. All I know is I don't have the budget for D.C. rent prices, and I really don't want to have to go back to the bank and take out yet another loan. I don't even know if any apartments nearby would let me take on a short-term lease at the last minute. I know Mom and Dad will let me come home, but…"

"It doesn't make sense to drag all your stuff to Idaho and back again," he finishes my thought.

"Exactly. And cross-country moves are expensive."

"Yeah, stay with us. We'll figure it out."

Alice's voice sounds further away. I imagine she's probably riding in the back seat as she pipes up. "Or you could stay somewhere you would not be forced to third wheel the newlyweds and listen to your own brother's nasty love noises. Take it from me, their usual third wheel. I'm sickened by these two every day, and I'm not even related to them. We'll find you a place. There are a few vacant apartments in Mike's old building. I was looking into it for myself, but I can't beat the free rent at my dad's place at the moment. Let me text Jake and get the building manager's contact info."

"Whatever they're charging, I'm sure North Bay is more affordable than D.C.," I say.

Danielle scoffs and protests. "Oh, like Shelley won't be exposed to way more 'love noises' in an apartment."

"Not from her own brother. I've heard the two of you. Believe me, Shelley, it's horrific," Alice interjects and makes exaggerated moaning sounds as I get a new text from her with the manager's name and number.

"But we won't charge her rent like they will," Danielle argues.

"Trust me, Shelley. You want some space from these two," Alice insists. "*So* much grunting."

Silly arguments aside, I actually do want space from my brother, if I can get it.

"Enough," Mike chimes in. "Shelley, come to North Bay. You can stay with us if you want, but the apartments are also a decent option. They have a few furnished units in the building. Now, ladies, could you cool it with the sound effects and talk about absolutely anything else with my sister, please?"

Furniture? I hadn't thought of that. My student housing came furnished, and I don't even own a bed, let alone a couch or a table.

"I appreciate both options," I tell them. "But Alice makes a fair point. I'll look into it and see if any short-term leases are available. Are you sure you guys won't mind me crashing your summer plans?"

"Are you kidding? This is going to be so fun! You can help me plan my next prank on Jake. Especially if you're his neighbor. Plus, with a lawyer on my side, now I'm going to win every argument with that punk."

"That punk" is probably the love of her life. We could all see how she was drooling over him at the wedding, and Jake is just as obsessed with her. Judging by the way she clung to him on the dance floor, I'd be willing to bet they've given in to their obvious chemistry at least once already.

"I'm not an attorney yet," I protest. "Only a student."

"Tomato, tamahto. I love this plan." I think I hear Alice clap.

"Sounds like you're spending the summer in North Bay then," my brother says.

"Looks that way."

"Cool. Okay, sis. Guess that means we'll be seeing you as soon as your semester ends. Let me know if you need help moving your stuff. I can recruit a few of the guys to come up there and help. And you're coming to Idaho for the game, right?"

I almost ask if Jordan will be one of his recruits for my move, but I stop myself. "Yeah. I'll be there to cheer you on. Thanks, Mikey. And thank you, Alice. You're a lifesaver. I did appreciate the offer to stay at the house, Danielle. But it sounds like the apartments are probably the safest bet for my delicate eardrums."

"No hard feelings. To be honest, we have enough roommate drama as it is with Honey around." Danielle laughs, and Mike barks out a noise I can only take as an agreement.

"I can imagine." I wonder what shenanigans Honey is pulling now. Maybe she's raiding their room for condoms after all.

I hang up, feeling relieved until I imagine Jordan's surprise if I show up in his building unannounced, and my stomach lurches. We haven't spoken since I hung up on him. I know I should reach out, but I haven't been able to bring myself to do that yet.

Talking to Mike and making a plan lifted some of the weight off my shoulders, but as soon as I enter my apartment and see the pile of clothes on the floor and my plethora of books and school supplies, the dread comes rushing back. I need to pack, and I'm running out of free days to get everything done. This weekend I'm flying back to Idaho, and when I return I won't have long before I need to be out of here. I don't know whether to laugh or cry. All I know is, ready or not, I'm moving to North Bay.

Chapter 17

Shelley

Standing at the end of the last row of chairs at Gate A10, I face away from the crowd so I can breathe and pat my pocket again to make sure I haven't misplaced my paper boarding pass. In all the chaos of packing, my apartment is basically still one giant pile of cardboard and clothing waiting for me to deal with it as soon as I get home from this trip. I was so worried I'd forget my pass or misplace it in the chaos, I slept in my clothes and put it in the pocket of my pink joggers.

Mandy always teases me for not using my phone to check in like every other twenty-something in this century, but I don't like trusting technology for things this important. What if I forget to charge my phone and it dies, or there's a Wi-Fi outage and I can't access my email? What if I drop my phone in a puddle or it crashes to the floor and shatters unexpectedly? I mean, now that I think about it, I guess half those things could also happen to a paper ticket, but this way I have a backup. Something about being able to hold a physical copy makes me feel like I have more control of the situation. And anything that gives me more control right now is a plus.

Airports are hell. The only thing worse than being here will be sitting in the actual plane, thousands of feet in the air with no way to get out. Could my family have possibly found a more inconvenient time to call us all home? I very much doubt it. I do not need this added stress in my life this close to finals.

I've already been to the bathroom three times, but I make another quick trip as they start to call the first boarding group for our plane. I have an assigned seat, and I know it will take a while before everyone is loaded in. Do four bathroom trips count as the kind of "suspicious activity" the announcements keep asking people to report? What if some well-meaning bystander reports me? Will they put me on a list? It's not my fault I have a nervous bladder, and I need to make sure it's completely empty before they shut the doors on this dubious aluminum torpedo. I'd rather not squeeze into the tiny, germy lavatory on the plane if I don't absolutely have to.

After I wash my hands and drag my rolling suitcase back to my gate, I park myself at the back of the line of passengers now boarding. We're moving slowly, and I take the opportunity to dig out my phone and send one last check-in text to the sisters group chat.

Me: *Boarding now. Be there in a few hours. Is someone picking me up or do I need to hail a cab?*

Mads: *You're such an old lady. But I'll get you. I'm tracking your flight. Can't wait to see your face!*

Mandy: *Seriously, who says "cab" anymore? See you soon. Hope you aren't next to a crying baby or anyone with B.O.*

Me: *Gee, thanks. Turning my phone off now. I love you brats. For some reason.*

I see Madison send through a pink heart before I switch my phone into airplane mode, just in time to hand my boarding pass to the flight attendant. As I walk down the long, rickety metal hall to the plane, I try to focus on taking deep breaths and plaster a determined look on my face. No reason for anyone else to know my legs feel like jelly and my stomach is threatening to bring back up the bagel I ate an hour ago. Maybe I should've asked Dr. Rappon to also prescribe something for my nerves to help me get through this flight.

Shaking my head at myself, I make my way to the back of the plane and find my row, then heave my suitcase into the overhead compartment before sinking down into the aisle seat and putting in my earbuds. This trip is already exhausting, and it has hardly started.

I love my family, but the cross-country trek whenever I want to see them in person is a lot. Unfortunately, there is no avoiding it this time. My mom is beside herself with excitement now that Virginia and Idaho both have major league teams. When she learned that Mikey would be playing one of his first Foxhounds games in our home state, less than an hour from the house, she started planning. Now it's a whole *Miller Family Event*. And those are not optional. My attendance is mandatory.

After everyone has boarded, there's still a hold-up of some sort. A handful of passengers seem frustrated as a flight attendant points between my row and another one closer to the middle of the plane. When she marches toward me, I remove one earbud to hear her say, "Ma'am, I hate to ask, but would you be willing to move your seat, by any chance? We're trying to rearrange some things in order for a mother to be able to sit with her four year old. Would you mind?"

I squeeze my lips together. I don't want to be a jerk. A kid that young shouldn't be forced to sit with strangers for hours. But the truth is I picked this seat on purpose, and I sort of do mind. I planned my trip carefully and followed all the rules. Why is this my problem? As I'm trying to decide on a polite but firm way to turn down the request, a familiar voice comes from behind her.

"I'll switch. The mom is already assigned to my row. The little guy can take my seat. I'll sit here."

"Jordan?" My stomach jumps.

"Thank you, sir. That's very kind." The flight attendant shuffles away to deal with the kid situation.

"Hey, Shelley. I decided to take your mom up on her invitation." He smiles too politely. It's the kind of smile you'd give in passing to the guy behind you in line at the store. Not the wider smile I'd become accustomed to, the one that assured me we were really friends. I miss the smile that reaches his eyes and makes them shine, like seeing me is a bright spot in his day. When his face returns to neutral, a twinge of disappointment joins the nerves already pooling in my belly, along with something warm and familiar, now that he's close enough for me to feel his body heat.

Why didn't my mother warn me he was coming?

Jordan seems guarded as he starts making small talk, and I wonder if he's as bothered as I am about the way our last phone call ended. I told myself I was overthinking, but maybe I wasn't. Did I hurt his feelings?

"I was curious if you'd be on this flight, but I didn't see you at the gate," he says. I'm sure that has something to do with my constant bathroom trips, but I'm not about to offer that information willingly.

"Looks like we're getting cozy for the next few hours." He points at the seat next to mine, and I stand to let him scoot into the middle chair. I hold my breath to avoid breathing in his intoxicating scent as he brushes past me.

A tiny bit of relief hits. I'm grateful I get to keep my carefully planned aisle seat, and I won't have to sit with a stranger or babysit a small child for the entire flight. But I still don't know if I'd say I'm happy to see him. The vibes between us are off, and I'm still irritated with him about all the mixed signals that annoyed me in the first place.

Once the seating arrangements are sorted and everyone, including the mother and child duo, is on board and buckled, we can finally pull away from the gate. As our flight crew begins the safety demonstration, I follow along and review the card in the seatback pocket in front of me, just like they suggest. I can sense Jordan's eyes on me, maybe mocking just a little, the same way I can feel the heat radiating off his leg, which is way too close to mine in these tight quarters. He's also hogging the armrest between us, so I have to work hard to squeeze my elbows into my sides so I don't touch him.

"*What?*" I say, defensively. "Safety is important to me."

"I can see that." He nods, an infuriating yet annoyingly adorable smirk playing with his lips. It's as though he doesn't want to let it out because he can see I'm being serious, but he can't help himself. "I'm impressed. I feel very well-protected with you as the fearless leader of row thirty-two."

I return the card to its place in the seat pocket and cross my arms. Like I said, this man is infuriating and annoying. Unfortunately for me, my ovaries haven't gotten the memo that they aren't supposed to find his playful smile adorable. My brows pinch as I attempt to ignore him while the captain informs us that we've been cleared for takeoff. As the plane roars to life and starts its assent, Jordan moves his hands to his lap to give me more space. I close my eyes and grip the armrest for dear life, whisper-counting to myself until I get to one hundred and the plane is well above the ground.

When I open my eyes again, I see Jordan glance at me sideways, but he doesn't say anything. He seems unaffected by the terrifying fact that we're defying gravity in a huge metal tube. I take long breaths in through my nose and inhale his warm, woodsy scent. It sends me straight back to the wedding, when we stood together facing the water with his jacket wrapped around my shoulders.

As the fasten seatbelts sign goes off, Jordan pulls a pouch from the backpack he stored under the seat in front of him. It looks like an extra-large pencil case. I'm intrigued when he unzips it and removes a crochet hook and a ball of yarn.

"What's that?"

He turns those disarming hazel eyes toward me again. "Just a hobby. I read that crocheting helps with dexterity and hand-eye coordination, so I picked it up a few years ago thinking it might improve my game. I make these." He reaches into the backpack again and produces a crocheted baseball with a silly, smiling face, then another one that looks angry. They're just like the one I saw on the TV console in his living room.

"You're allowed to bring those needles on a plane?"

"Yep. They're fine with crochet hooks, especially the plastic ones. We do it all the time. A couple of the other guys on the team started making these, too. Now we all do it when we have long bus or plane rides. We hand them out to kids in the crowd when we do community events."

I'd assumed the first one I saw was a gift from a fan, but now I can picture a bus full of ball players surrounded by yarn, happily stitching silly faces onto their crocheted baseballs. Whatever was left of my annoyance melts away as a huge smile breaks out on my face. "Okay, I love this. It might be the best thing I've ever heard."

Jordan chuckles. "Here, you can have this one." He hands me a baseball with pink stitching and eyelashes meant to rival a Hollywood starlet. There are tiny red hearts stitched on the cheeks to look like blush.

"Thank you." I take the gift and squeeze it lightly, another layer of my stress lifting. When I look at him again, Jordan's finally wearing his genuine friendship smile.

"Do you want me to show you how to make one?" he asks. "Fun fact: Crocheting also lowers cortisol. And you seem a little stressed. It might be a good distraction until we land?"

"What exactly makes you think I need a distraction?"

He only raises his eyebrows and gives me a knowing look in response. Guess I'm not hiding my nerves as well as I hoped.

"Fine. I'm not the best flyer. So, yes. Please." I nod and he takes another hook from the bag, untangling it from some loose strands of yarn. His hand brushes mine as he gives me the supplies, and a familiar tingle runs up my spine. I swallow and try to ignore it as I say, "Thanks" one more time.

Jordan shows me how to start a row and briefly explains the stitch I need. After a few practice tries, I start to get the hang of it and follow his lead to continue my stitches into a row. Having something to focus on lessens the tension and makes it a bit easier to breathe the thin, recirculating cabin air.

"Do you know how to make anything else?" I ask out of curiosity, looping the yarn around my hook like he taught me. My project is looking pretty pathetic so far, hanging limp in my hand with uneven spaces between the stitches. I don't see a world in which this mess of knots is going to turn into one of those cute little smiling baseballs, but I'm still grateful to have something to do with my hands, and for the excuse to avoid eye contact while we talk.

"Sorry to disappoint, but I only learned one stitch so I could make these. I guess this pattern could be a tennis ball too, if we change the color of the yarn." He turns to me, and I'm grateful to see him looking happy again. "We could probably make a potholder. Do you want to try that?"

"Nah. I won't get any use out of a potholder. Not a big cook over here, remember?"

"I do remember," he says, letting his voice soften enough to feel like a hug before he clears his throat. "Let me show you how to make a baseball."

I follow his lead. With my hands occupied, I'm finally comfortable enough to tell him, "I have some news. They're doing repair work on my graduate housing, so I'll be in North Bay for the summer. I'm renting an apartment in your building. But I'm not stalking you, I promise."

"Sounds like something a stalker would say," he teases. Then he adds, "Mike already told me, but thanks for the heads-up."

For the remainder of the flight, we work on our projects. Hours pass, but I'm so absorbed in the task that I'm surprised to hear the announcement when we're descending and need to put away our belongings. My fingers brush against his again, and the familiar heat runs through me at the contact as I hand back the yarn and hook.

"That was fun."

It's true, and I'm surprised I've been able to enjoy myself as much as I have while we are hurdling through the atmosphere at unnatural speeds.

"It was. And, hey, we're good, right? I know we left things a little awkward the last time we talked."

"Yeah. We're good." I nod.

Jordan zips everything back into his backpack and pushes it under the seat in front of him again. Then he leans back into his own chair and turns his head to face me.

His eyes crinkle at the corners when he offers me another real smile and turns his palm up on the armrest in a silent offer to hold my hand for the landing. I link my fingers through his, grateful for the gesture, and hold my new blushing baseball gift tightly in my other hand while I try not to squeeze Jordan too hard or dig my nails into him as the engines get louder.

When I flinch at a clunking sound, he drops his shoulder and leans toward me until our upper arms are touching. His lips are so close I feel his warm breath against my cheek when he whispers, "That was just the landing gear. We're okay."

I nod and swallow, but I must not look convincingly calm yet, because his other hand comes down to cover where we're already joined. His thumb traces small circles over my knuckle, and every cell in my body redirects its attention to that tiny point of contact.

Who could form a single coherent thought when Jordan Wagner is casually stroking their skin in this minuscule interaction that probably means nothing to him, yet means everything to me? Because, just like in the hotel room, I know he sees. I don't have to say anything. Jordan can read me effortlessly. It's like my soul was written in a language he speaks fluently, even though it's indecipherable to everyone else on the planet. With him I don't feel strange, or out of place, or like I'm too much. I can just…feel. I feel so much it's overwhelming and causes me to pull my hand away.

As soon as I lose the contact, I wish I had it back, but Jordan seems unfazed as he looks toward the window.

"All the farmland sort of looks like a big quilt from up here," he muses. "Are you excited to be home?"

"Sure." I nod because I see what he means. Large patches of land are plowed into straight, rectangular patches for crops, and they're harvested at different times, so some areas are green, while others are yellow or brown. From our overhead view, they really do look like squares in a patchwork quilt. For a minute my mind wanders to the old blankets my mom keeps draped over the chairs in our living room.

As crazy as my family can be, I miss them, and I'm excited to see them all again. I know it hasn't been long since we all saw each other at the wedding, but it's different on home turf. I want to hang out with my sisters in our own space, eat Mom's pancakes for breakfast, and relax under my tree in the backyard.

When we're safely on the ground again, Jordan shoulders his backpack and pulls both of our suitcases down from the overhead compartment before he hands me my bag. "Ready?"

"Lead the way," I say as I follow him down the aisle.

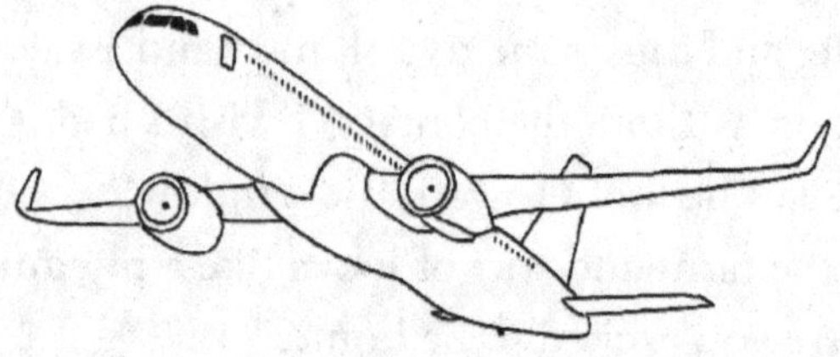

"Lead the way," I say

Chapter 18

Jordan

I bring my fist up to cover my yawn. It was a cross-country flight and we're in a new time zone, but the time difference has given us a few of those hours back. So even though it's early in the afternoon, it's already been a long day. At this rate, I'll be lucky to stay awake through the second inning of the Foxhounds game tonight.

When I called Mike's mom to let her know my schedule was going to allow me to fly out and catch the Idaho game, she acted like I told her she'd won the lottery. I said I'd book a hotel, but Mrs. Miller wouldn't hear of it. She insisted I stay in Mike's old room, since he'll be bunking with the team and Danielle stayed back to help Alice through a family emergency. I believe Mrs. Miller's exact words were, "Don't be ridiculous. You're family, Jordan. Why on Earth would you pay those crazy hotel fees when there's an empty bed and a hot meal waiting for you right here?" Who am I to argue with logic like that?

Madison was nice enough to pick us up at the airport and drive us to the house, and Mandy is up front with her. I'm in the back seat with Shelley squeezed in next to me. Much like our seats on the plane, the small space in the back of this sedan wasn't designed for two tall bodies. Between all our grazing touches on the flight and the way her knee is lightly knocking into mine every time we hit a bump in the road, my nerve endings might as well be live wires. Every cell in my body is on high alert when she's near me.

"Home sweet home," Madison says as the car slows.

I've never been to Mike's parents' place before this trip, but I know the Millers well now. They're nice people with a real all-American aesthetic. So far, from my limited exposure to their home state, Idaho seems very…blond. When the car pulls up to their house, I'm not surprised to see the decorative seasonal flag on the porch or the hanging flower baskets. Mrs. Miller is already waiting by the mailbox, waving.

"I share my location with her," Shelley explains, unbuckling her seatbelt. "She was probably watching us the whole time." She rolls her eyes, but I think it's nice to have someone excited to see you come home.

I exit the car and grab both of our bags out of the trunk, setting them down on the curb while Shelley's mom greets her. Then Mrs. Miller approaches me with her arms spread wide, looking for a hug.

"Jordan!" She reaches up to wrap her arms tightly around my neck. "I'm so glad you decided to stay with us this weekend." She plants a kiss on my cheek, then uses her thumb to wipe away the lipstick mark.

"Thank you for having me." I offer her another small squeeze. She nods and pulls away to reach up again to pat my cheek.

"Go ahead upstairs. Shelley can show you to your room. I'll let Dad know you're all here," she says. "He's with a client, but he'll be finished with work in a few hours."

Mrs. Miller heads in through the front door, and I grab our bags as Shelley and her sisters show me to a side entrance leading up to the family's quarters. Mike's told me about this place, but the old three-story Gothic-style home is bigger than I imagined. It looks like it's a remodeled church. Back in Virginia, a property like this would probably be called an estate. According to Mike, it's been in their family for four generations. The main floor on the ground level serves as a funeral parlor. It's a large open space that can be used for services, plus a small office, a powder room, and a private mourning room.

There's a wooden staircase, and I follow behind Shelley, my eyes zeroed in on her swaying hips as we ascend each step. The second and third floors are set up like any other house, with the lower level being the main living area. There's a kitchen, dining area, bathroom, and den. The bedrooms and two additional bathrooms are up on the third floor. It's a hike, but we make our way up all the wide, winding stairs, and Shelley points to an ornate wooden door on the left.

"That's you."

"Cool. Thanks." I hand over her suitcase, and she takes it into a room across the hall, closing her door and leaving me staring at the carved wooden slab for a few seconds longer than necessary.

Regaining my senses, I turn and toss my stuff onto the bottom mattress of my best friend's childhood bunk bed. There's a framed family photo sitting on the dresser, reminding me exactly how much of an asshole I would be if I tried anything with his little sister. But the truth is, I don't know if I have the strength to stay away much longer.

I've tried. I thought these feelings would fade into the background if I ignored them, but they've only grown. Spending the day with her on the plane and the overwhelming need I had to comfort her when she was afraid only confirmed it. The pull Shelley has on me is stronger than a rip current, and I'm getting tired of fighting to swim against the tide.

Mrs. Miller calls up to us, "I'm sure you're both exhausted from the flight, but don't forget to set an alarm if you decide to take a nap. We're leaving for the game in a few hours."

A nap sounds like a great idea. I nod off almost immediately and don't wake up until I hear the girls arguing and shuffling around in the bathroom as they fight over the mirror.

When I step into the hall, I almost collide with Shelley as she backward-stomps out of the bathroom, growling at her sisters. "I said I needed five more minutes."

"You can curl your hair anywhere there's an outlet! I need to get in here," Mandy fires back.

Shelley turns, still not seeing me, and I grab her elbow to keep her steady. The contact takes her by surprise, and she gasps, tripping over her own feet. Before she falls, I manage to wrap an arm around her waist and pull her close to me.

"Steady now."

"I'm fine," she whispers. "You can let go."

It's harder than it should be, but I manage to loosen my hold enough for her to slip out.

She's wearing a pink Foxhounds jersey tied up on the side and tight bike shorts that hug her thighs. The five on her back is her brother's number. I know Mrs. Miller had matching jerseys custom-made for the whole family as soon as Mike signed his contract. Of course Shelley should be wearing a Foxhounds jersey tonight. But I have to clear my throat and tap my fist against my chest because there's an uncomfortable burning inside me. New fantasy unlocked: Before I retire, I want to see her in my jersey.

"Let's get a move on!" Mr. Miller calls from downstairs, so we all file out of the house and into the family minivan to head over to the stadium.

The league added five additional teams this year, and there's a low hum of excitement in the air from the minute we pull into the parking area. Everything is new. The stadium, the lights, the vendors, down to the athletes themselves. Idaho is here for it. It seems like every person in the county will be heading into the stands tonight. Tour buses from big companies and passenger vans painted with church logos pull up alongside campers and pick-up trucks for the tailgate.

Mr. Miller opens the trunk of the minivan and gets to work setting up a pop-up tent while Mrs. Miller unloads a crockpot of sloppy joe meat and a foil pan filled with chocolate chip cookie bars. We share dinner with some friendly parking lot neighbors who offer chili, hot dogs, and JELL-O shots while Mike's mom proudly tells everyone within earshot that her son is playing tonight. Finally, it's time to head into the stadium for the game.

"How many of those cookie bars did you have?" Shelley whispers as she slides up next to me. It's windy tonight, and she's wearing a light jacket over her jersey. "I stole a few extras. They're in my pocket for emergencies."

I lean close to whisper back. "I won't tell. Pretty sure I had like five. Think your mom will give me her recipe?"

She scoffs playfully. "My mom share her cookie bar recipe? Not a chance. She won't even give it to Mandy."

The fielders are starting to take their positions, and Shelley cups her hands around her mouth to shout, "That's my brother!" as we take our seats. Mike looks up and smiles, nodding in our direction.

It's a low-scoring game. Even I can admit, baseball is a lot more fun to play than it is to watch.

During Mike's at-bat in the top of the third inning, he makes contact but it's a pop-up easily caught by Idaho's pitcher. As he returns to the dugout, Shelley says she needs to use the bathroom, and her sisters decide to tag along, vacating their seats.

"I'll come with you," I say as I get up to follow them.

After using the facilities, Mandy and Maddy come out of the restroom together and head back to the stands. Not wanting Shelley to be left behind, I hang back. It only takes a minute for her to reappear.

"Sorry. There was a line. You didn't have to wait."

I shrug and tuck my hands into the back pockets of my jeans. "Did you want to get some cotton candy or something?"

She laughs. "Are you seriously still hungry? I know I said I could always eat, but I think I'm good after that tailgate. And I'm not letting you pay twenty bucks for cotton candy when I have pocket cookies." She pats her jacket pocket and effortlessly pulls a chuckle out of me before she gets more serious. "But I do want to take a walk and see if I can find a quiet corner for a second. It's a little overstimulating in here, if I'm being honest."

"Can I join you, or do you want some space?"

"Sure. Come on. Let's explore a little."

It doesn't take us long to discover the stadium actually has a designated Quiet Room behind thick glass doors. The signs on the walls invite anyone who needs a break to come in and get out of the noise for a few minutes. There are headphones lining the left wall and a bin of dark sunglasses available, along with a small plaque that explains how everything is sterilized between each use. Shelley runs her fingers over the sign but doesn't take any of the items they're offering.

"This is cool," she muses. "It must help a lot of kids. I wish stuff like this had been around when I was younger."

"It's nice," I agree.

We're the only people here, and she sits down on a long vinyl bench, which is upholstered in the orange and yellow Idaho Talons colors. Shelley leans her head back against the wall, closing her eyes and inhaling a deep breath through her nose. This window into her private moment makes me feel like I'm intruding, but I can't take my eyes off her.

"Come sit." She pats the space to her right, eyes still closed. I cross the room to accept the invitation, sitting down next to her.

Shelley pivots toward me, and her eyes open while she lifts to tuck one leg under herself. "It was really nice of you to come out to support Mike. It must be hard for you to take time away from your team during the season."

My focus falls to her lips, which are painted with a shimmery pink gloss that steals my attention. I'm so tired of fighting this.

"I have a confession. I may have had an ulterior motive for agreeing to this particular trip."

"Oh? Do tell." Those pink lips turn up on one side in a crooked half-smile.

She's so close. Our legs are touching, and with no barrier like an armrest between us, we're even closer here now than we were on the plane or out in the stands.

"Your mom called me family, and that's sort of my kryptonite."

Her smile widens to brighten her whole face, and it warms me from the inside. "Well, she's right. You're stuck with us now."

"I could get used to that."

She nods. "Good."

"Shelley?" I take a risk and lean in until my lips are next to her ear.

"Hmm?" She tilts her head, maybe subconsciously, exposing more of her neck, and I have no choice but to inhale. I don't know the first thing about how to tell which flower it is, but her perfume smells fresh and floral like a damn bouquet.

"Are you getting sick of fighting this pull between us? Because I am," I admit.

Her soft inhale is the only hint of surprise she offers before her tone shifts to a sultry tease. "So don't."

And there goes the last tiny fragment of my willpower. All the reasons we said we shouldn't do this are still true. But I'm tired of pretending I'm strong enough to deny this.

"If you don't want me to kiss you now, you need to tell me," I repeat her words from the hotel, praying she doesn't stop it like I did that night. I'll get up now and walk away if she needs me to. It will be hard, but I'll do it, if that's what she wants.

Her face turns toward mine again, agonizingly slowly.

"I'll never tell you not to kiss me, Jordan."

That's all I need to hear to close the final inch of space between us and pull her into me. One hand finds her waist while the other tangles in her hair, and I inhale her like she's oxygen while our mouths explore, tentatively at first, then with more fervor until she's tugging gently on my bottom lip with her teeth, fisting her hands in my shirt.

Still clinging tightly to the fabric, she pulls away hesitantly. Her eyes are closed when she starts to ask, "What about—"

"I was wrong," I tell her quickly. "I'm sorry. About everything. I know it's complicated, Shelley, but I should have put you first. Mike won't like it, but you were right. He doesn't get a say here. I'd really like to try—"

Her mouth is on mine again before I finish the thought. After a few more magical minutes, she sighs contentedly and pulls back just enough to look at me while she flattens her hand on my chest. "And here I thought my pocket cookies were going to be the sweetest part of tonight."

I smile and put my hand over hers. "If you're telling me I rank higher than those cookie bars, I'm taking it as the highest compliment."

"You should. But we need to get back out there. They must be wondering where we are."

"Okay. How do you want to play this?"

"I think we should keep it to ourselves for now. Tonight isn't about us."

I nod. As much as I'd love to claim her as mine in front of the world, I can understand Shelley wanting to take this slow and see where it goes.

"Yeah. That's probably a good idea." I squeeze her hand and steal one more kiss before I escort her back to the stands, where we sit inches apart, next to her parents, while I try to focus on the game and pretend I didn't just sneak off to make out with their daughter.

The night sky is dark over the field, but my whole world is suddenly brighter.

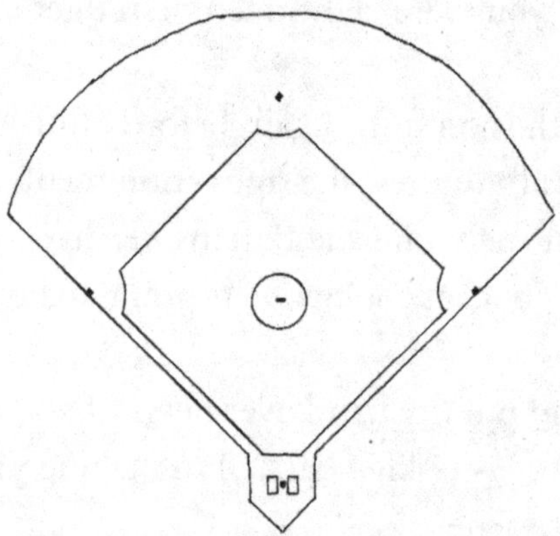

Chapter 19

Shelley

"Stalking him much?" Maddy giggles as she brushes past me in the hall, where I'm waiting for Jordan to get out of the shower.

"I was going to show him the way to the kitchen," I offer the lamest of all excuses.

"Right. Sure." She gives me an exaggerated nod.

"He's our guest. I'm trying to be nice."

"Whatever you say." She bounds down the stairs, calling back, "But if you miss breakfast while you stand there drooling, don't expect me to save you any bacon."

It was almost impossible to sit next to Jordan for the remainder of the game last night and act like nothing happened, but somehow, we managed. We snuck in one more goodnight kiss before bed, then we went to our separate rooms. I think my sisters might be starting to suspect something's up, but at least my parents still seem to be blissfully in the dark about the turn things have taken between me and their house guest.

When Jordan emerges, my mouth goes dry as my eyes scan from the dark tee stretched across his shoulders up to his hazel eyes and damp curls.

"Sorry. Did you need to get in here?" He motions toward the doorway with his thumb.

"No. I thought I could finally take you to breakfast. I know this great little restaurant called My Parents' Kitchen. There's not even a bill for us to fight over." I smile and he returns one of his own.

"Sounds like an offer I can't refuse. Lead the way."

Dad stands at the kitchen counter, picking blueberries off the fruit platter he set out. "Oh, Shelley, I forgot to tell you. The crew is coming to remove the sycamore out back next Tuesday. We had another arborist come out to look, but it can't be saved. Too bad, really. I'll miss looking out there and seeing that thing. Remember how you kids used to climb it? You spent hours in that tree." He continues chewing as though he hasn't just casually dropped a bomb on me.

My heart clenches, and I blink a few times in a failing effort to keep my eyes dry. It would be silly to cry over a tree, but it feels like I'm getting bad news about an old friend. I swallow down the unwelcome bubble of sadness and nod. "That's terrible. I love that tree."

"Well, then you better go out back and say your goodbyes, because I'm afraid it won't be here the next time you come home."

"I'll make sure to get out there before I leave. And Dad? Can I borrow your car? I made plans to meet Jo Wilson at Cozy Kitchen in a little while."

"Sure, kiddo. Maybe I can convince Jordan to throw a few darts with me in the basement while you're gone."

"I'd like that," Jordan tells my dad before turning to me. "Have fun with your friend."

"I will. We have a lot to talk about." I wonder if he remembers Jo's name from my voice memo. The way he nods and quickly takes a sip of orange juice rather than respond makes me think he probably does.

An hour later, I arrive at the restaurant to see Jo has already saved us a table. She waves me over and stands to give me a quick hug when I reach her.

"Shelley! How are you?" She's cut her hair since the last time I saw her. It's grazing her shoulders in a long bob.

"Hi, Jo. It's been a while."

"Way too long. What brought you back to Idaho?"

We take our seats across from each other as I explain, "Mike's in the majors now, I don't know if you heard. He had a game at the new stadium last night."

"Oh, that's amazing. Pass along my congratulations, will you?"

"Sure." Not wanting to spend too much time talking about my brother, I turn the conversation to her. "Are you still running?"

"When I can find the time," she says in the affirmative, and we spend a few minutes catching up as we both order the hot chocolate with whipped cream and get a mega muffin to split, just like the old days. It isn't long before our server delivers our treats. Jo tells me about the Turkey Trot she ran on Thanksgiving alongside a few of our mutual acquaintances. I nibble at my half of the muffin slowly before I take a breath and brave asking the questions I really came to speak to her about.

"I saw your published article, speaking of congratulations being in order. I'm so excited about your work. I was hoping you might be able to offer some insight into my own…situation." I glance down at the jeans currently doing their best to hide the traitor otherwise known as my vulva. "As it turns out, I'm one of the women you were talking about. I've seen a few doctors, and I'm trying some new meds. But do you have any general advice?"

Jo sets down the spoon she was using to scoop her whipped cream and reaches a hand across the table while she looks at me. "First, let me say you're doing the right thing by talking about it. A lot of women struggle to find the courage to take that step, so kudos. It can be hard to say out loud."

"No kidding."

She goes on, "I'm sure the pros you've already seen have given you the best advice there is, which is to see if you can find pleasure in other aspects of the experience and take your mind off the idea of the climax being the end game."

I sigh and nod. "Yeah, that seems to be everyone's go-to answer."

"That's because it's true. But I know it can be frustrating," she admits.

"I'm also still on the same meds I've been taking since sophomore year. It's a stimulant for ADHD. I can send you a photo of the label if it helps."

"I'm not a medical doctor, so I don't know that I'd be much help there."

I wave her concern away with my hand. "I actually just had an appointment with my psychiatrist, and we're going to lower the dose, then try something else if it doesn't work. I was also offered an estrogen cream at the gynecologist, which I do think is helping. And we talked a little bit about a shot. Do you know anything about that? It seems really expensive, and I'm not sure I'm ready to go the needles up the hoo-ha route."

Jo lets out a small laugh. "I can understand that. To be honest, I haven't seen enough research yet to be able to form an opinion about the shots."

"That's the same thing my doctor said." All these choices still have me confused.

"No matter which route you choose, don't be afraid to speak up for yourself. As far as any of your doctors are concerned, it's their literal job to help bodies function the way they should and make sure the right medication reaches the people who need it. That's what you pay them for."

She's right. I know that, but it's still mortifying and frustrating. And it's hard to prioritize something that seems as trivial as getting myself more turned on. It's not like I'm going to spontaneously combust if I can't come, even if sometimes it feels like I might.

"Yeah, that's true," I concede, then I sigh again. "Other than adjusting my meds, I still don't know what else I can do. I shouldn't have bothered you with this. I'm sorry. It's just been so hard. And I'm kind of seeing someone now, so I'm worried it could become a bigger problem."

"Don't you dare apologize," she scolds, picking up her mug and blowing on her hot chocolate. "Taking steps to adjust your meds is huge! I'm so happy to hear you're trying that. You aren't bothering me at all. It's also *my* job to help women prioritize their own health and happiness. Your decision is personal, and whatever you decide will be the right choice for you. Also? Just in case you need to hear someone say it, female orgasms *are* important, even if they don't always get the recognition they deserve. You know this is my soapbox." She takes on a more serious tone to tell me, "Seeking satisfaction is, in itself, a good enough reason to ask for help, but there are also a lot of medical reasons it's valuable."

"Yeah, I know," I say, still not fully believing it.

"It's true. Orgasms improve the quality of your sleep, increase your immune function, contribute to pain relief, and have tons of other health benefits in addition to your sexual satisfaction. Some people think they might even help improve fertility. This is not a superficial thing. Don't let anyone make you feel like it is. Women's health is important, and more people should be talking about it like this. I'm glad you called. I'm here for you."

"Thanks, Jo. I think I really needed to hear that."

"Anytime. It's amazing you're taking these steps for yourself. Truly. I'm proud of you. Let me know if I can do anything else. I need to run soon. I have plans with my mom this afternoon, but I'm so glad we got to catch up."

"Me, too. This was really helpful. I appreciate it."

"Anytime. And tell your sisters I said hi."

"Will do. Thanks again."

"Sure thing. Keep in touch, okay?"

"Absolutely." I give her quick goodbye hug and pick up the check before heading home. Finally getting to talk to someone who understands is validating, and listening to Jo has me feeling more positive about my body and my choices than I have in a long time.

Chapter 20

Shelley

The old sycamore tree behind my parents' house has been my favorite thinking spot for as long as I can remember. The long, thick branches cradle me perfectly, once I finally wrestle my way up to them. Tree climbing does not appear to be a skill that translates well from youth into adulthood. But with only a few scraped knuckles and some leaves in my hair, I manage to settle into the crook of a low, sturdy branch. I take a moment to catch my breath and savor the cool spring breeze. I love the way it glides lightly over my skin when I'm up here.

"Thought I might find you out here." The deep vibrations of Jordan's words cause an unfamiliar kind of heat to pool low in my belly as my body remembers how it felt when he finally kissed me yesterday.

"You caught me. How did the dart game go?"

"Your dad thinks I let him win, but he crushed me, fair and square." He hoists himself into the tree like it's nothing. As he gracefully swings himself onto the branch next to mine, I cringe and hope he didn't witness the embarrassing amount of awkward maneuvers required for me to do the same.

Sitting in the tree with me, his presence is overwhelming in a way that makes me nervous, but not intimidated. He's familiar and exciting all at once, like a brand-new season of my favorite TV show. Sharing space with Jordan is easy and natural, and I don't take that for granted. It's not something I experience with most people.

I stretch out my legs and lean back against the bark, letting the tree's rough texture ground me as it presses its way through my clothes and into my skin. I offer Jordan a smile, which he returns easily. He sits on his branch like it's any other chair, with his legs dangling over the edge and one hand lazily resting on a higher branch.

"Penny for your thoughts?"

"Apparently, my thoughts aren't worth much to you," I tease.

"Okay. Then a mint condition Ted Williams rookie card for your thoughts?"

"Is that worth a lot?"

"Let's just say, if I had one, I wouldn't still be living with a roommate."

I shrug. "You can keep the imaginary card this time. I wasn't really thinking about anything in particular. It's kind of a jumbled mess of stuff up here." I point at my head. "But I do love this tree, and it will be sad to see it go."

His understanding comes in the form of a low hum, but I want him to keep talking. I like the way his voice cuts through the chaos in my brain. I wish he'd tell me I'm not the mess I think I am. More than anything, I want to know he isn't looking at Mike's little sister right now. I want his reassurance that last night was real and our kiss meant something to him. I want to know for sure he sees *me*, which is odd because usually I go out of my way to avoid being seen and keep my mask on for the world. But with Jordan it's different, and I'm frustrated when he remains still and quiet, looking up into the higher branches and watching the clouds float by above the leaves.

"Is it good to be home?" He surprises me with his question.

"Sure. It's nice." My answer is genuine. I love my family. But maybe he can tell it's bittersweet for me to return. Before I left for college, the last few years I spent in this house were the hardest my family ever had to endure, and a lot of unpleasant memories rise to the surface when I come home.

"But?"

I want to be honest with him. "Everything was so chaotic here all the time when I was younger, and I always felt like I was trying to play by rules I didn't understand. When he was using, my parents were preoccupied with Mike because they had to be. They were always fighting about how to handle him. And the rest of us were left to fend for ourselves." Which meant *I* was fending for all of us. "I get that it was necessary, but I wished things were different. I wanted things to make sense. I wanted rules. And I wanted adults and a big brother who followed those rules. Maybe it's naïve and idealistic, but that's where my head was when I decided to start studying family law."

"I think the world could use a little more idealism," he offers. "It's admirable that you wanted to take the trauma and create something good from it."

"Maybe. But there I go again, making it all about me." Sharing with him feels more natural than breathing. Without even trying, Jordan manages to collect the secrets I normally guard so carefully.

"Enough about me. Tell me something about you no one else knows," I say, shifting the conversation back to him.

Jordan's quiet for a long moment, thinking before he says, "I watch horror movies when I need to cheer up."

"Oh? Please say more."

"I don't think I've told anyone this, but when I'm upset or sad, I usually sit by myself and watch a scary movie. The gorier the better. They make me happy. Which I realize sounds incredibly messed up."

"I'm reserving judgment until you tell me why. Don't worry. At the moment, it's only giving light red flag vibes," I tease. "Please explain."

"It started when I was young. My mom had this DVD collection she was so proud of. She bought like a hundred movies for twenty bucks back when video stores were going out of business." He repositions his body on the branch. "She wouldn't allow me to watch them, but I was alone in our apartment so much that no one was around to stop me or see what I was doing. So, one day I thought I was being rebellious, and I watched The Exorcist."

"How old were you?"

"Too young. Maybe seven or eight? But the thing is, it didn't scare me. There was so much real-world stuff to be afraid of every day, like parents getting arrested, or eviction notices on the door, or running out of food. The idea of levitating or having my head spin seemed silly in comparison. I thought it was funny grown-ups could actually be scared of something like that. I guess it made me feel brave to watch it and not be affected."

My chest squeezes at the idea of little Jordan being forced to navigate big, adult-sized challenges while he learned how to channel his courage all alone in his living room.

"So, I kept watching them," he continues. "And I learned most of the things the world said were scary were totally unrealistic. Strangers with chainsaws were way less believable than the stuff that actually scared me. Now I guess I associate those movies with feeling safe, which sounds weird, I know."

"No, it doesn't. I'm glad you found something that worked for you," I try to reassure him. "Thank you for telling me."

"Does this mean I get another one of your secrets?" he asks, a hint of hope lacing his question, giving me the impression that maybe, just maybe, he values these conversations as much as I do.

I hesitate because I only have one secret left, and it involves his best friend. But I nod and let out a shallow breath, knowing it's probably not much of a secret anyway. "Sometimes I still resent my brother for what he put our family through. I know it's not fair because he's done so much to change. But I can't help how I feel."

Jordan nods, slowly. "Mike's told me a little bit about how bad things got for a while, but I've never met *that* guy. I haven't seen that side of him."

"I know. And I love how he's been able to rebuild his life in North Bay." I do. I love my brother, and I'm so proud of him and everything he's been able to accomplish. He did the work and made amends. He has apologized so sincerely, so many times. "I forgave him a long time ago, but it doesn't mean it's easy to forget. It's hard to watch someone you love self-destruct right in front of you and know you can't do anything to help. Watching them become a different person changes a kid. Fundamentally."

"I get it." Jordan's somber tone tells me he really does understand. From what I know about his parents, I believe him.

"I love Mikey. He's my brother, first and always. But..." I clear my throat to try to rid myself of the lump that is forming in my airway. "He was the reason I had to grow up early, you know? Somebody had to make sure everything else wasn't falling apart."

"I do know. I can definitely relate to feeling like you had to grow up before you were ready."

I sniffle and nod, turning away to hide the tear rolling down my cheek. "I know you can. Thanks for listening. I haven't really been able to talk about it with anyone before."

"Of course. I've...I've never really done this either. It's nice to have someone to talk to about this stuff."

It really is.

"Tell me something else," he whispers.

"I'm neurodivergent," I say quietly. "But you've probably already figured that out."

He nods again, just once. "I like the way your brain works."

"Thanks, but I need medicine for it to function effectively, and that's not the case for everyone. Hence, the necessity of the label. I definitely have ADHD. I'm not sure if I'm on the spectrum. I think I might be, but it's hard for adult women to get diagnosed. I guess it might not change much for me, but sometimes I think it might be nice to have confirmation."

"Yeah, I'm learning labels can be helpful sometimes. I'm still working on finding the right words to describe myself, too. Am I allowed to ask about the meds? You don't have to tell me." He shifts to lean back against the tree trunk.

"It's okay. I brought it up. I've been on medication since I was about sixteen. School was never an issue for me, but when I was learning how to drive, my mom was worried that my being easily distracted was too dangerous. And the pills really do seem to make a difference for me." They make it easier to focus. I think more clearly and feel more like myself when I'm on meds. "There are some side effects, though."

"Like what?"

I sigh. "The last time I spoke with my psychiatrist, I brought up my little *problem*. Turns out it's pretty common. So, we're going to try a different medicine. My other doctor also put me on an estrogen cream. Apparently, there's also a shot some people try, but I decided not to go that far."

"Really?" He sounds surprised. "I had no idea that was a thing. Do you feel a little better knowing there was a real medical reason?"

I mull it over. "I thought I would. I appreciate the doctors taking me seriously. But I'm still frustrated that the issue hasn't completely gone away. I think it's improving some with the med changes, but I guess I won't really know until, well, you know. I'll have to test that hypothesis in the field, so to speak." I wiggle my eyebrows and he chuckles. "If switching my pills and adding the cream doesn't work, it could still be a problem with my body just being outright defective."

Jordan scoffs. "Your body is a lot of things, Shelley. Defective isn't one of them."

"Is that so?' My tone turns flirty. "Do tell what all these other things are."

He lets out an exaggerated groan and shakes his head. "Nope. You won't be getting it out of me that easily. Wouldn't want you to get a big head over there."

"Oh, come on. Indulge me. You don't know what it's like to feel your own body betray you like this." I throw an arm over my eyes dramatically, but Jordan reaches over and gently lifts it off again.

"I think I actually do know a little something about that. And you're right, it sucks. But your body belongs in a goddamn art museum. I haven't stopped thinking about it since watching you strip in front of that mirror, you little minx."

"I can't believe I did that." I turn away to cover my blush, but then curiosity about something else he said gets the better of me. "What do you mean you know the feeling?" I tilt my head. "Being demi doesn't make you broken, Jordan."

"I'm starting to realize that," he says, eyes shining with sincerity. Then he taps a finger against his bad elbow. "I was actually talking about this. My arm probably isn't going to work exactly the way I'd like it to ever again. It's throbbing a little right now just from pulling myself up into this tree. I know I should be grateful I had a chance to play ball for a living—and I am—and I'm also glad the injury wasn't worse. But it's still taking away something I worked hard for. It's okay to admit when something feels really shitty."

"Exactly!" I move a little too quickly and gasp as I almost lose my balance on the branch before I catch myself. Jordan scoots closer and reaches out to keep me from falling. When I'm confident I'm steady again, I tell him, "I hate knowing my body doesn't work the way it's supposed to. It makes me feel like such a failure."

He leans forward and crooks a finger under my chin and raises my face so my eyes meet his as he tells me, "You're not."

If only it were as easy to believe as he makes it seem. But he should know it's not.

"You're not either. You know that, right?" I blink at him. Apparently, we both have our fair share of issues to sort through.

"I'm working on believing it, too," he promises. He takes a long breath before he says, "Shelley, I want you to know I'm serious when I say you're gorgeous, and I do want you. But relationships are complicated for me, even without all the other concerns we're piling on top of this. So, this thing between us, whatever it is, it might not look exactly like it does for other people. We get to define it."

"I'd like that. And I hope you don't feel like I'm pressuring you either."

He huffs out a laugh. "I wouldn't have flown all the way across the country if I didn't want to be here. Once I'm in, I'm all in."

And with that, the butterflies are back.

"But I do need you to promise me you'll take your time and really think this through before we do anything we can't take back. You have more to lose here, Shelley."

I don't want my brother to be a factor in this. I shake my head. "Mike's not going to—"

"I'm not only thinking about Mike. I'm thinking of you. You still have your whole career in front of you, and you need to focus on school. I don't have any of that, and I don't want to mess any of it up for you. I don't want to be the distraction that throws you off the path you worked hard to create for yourself. But I'm also not strong enough to fight this anymore."

"You're so much more than a distraction, Jordan." I climb over to his thicker branch, and he leans against the trunk of the tree while I cup his face in my hands.

I'm in big trouble. I have it bad for my brother's best friend, and all he's offered so far are a handful of stolen kisses and a few honest conversations. If Jordan gives me more, I know I won't be able to stop myself from falling for him. Hard. And it's more than a little bit terrifying. But when I kiss him again, nothing else seems to matter.

Chapter 21

Shelley

"Let me in, you asshats," I whisper to my sisters through gritted teeth as I pull at the locked doorknob of our shared childhood bedroom. It doesn't budge. This is their revenge for yesterday when Mandy thought I took too long to let her into the bathroom. My sisters conspire with each other from the other side. Their voices are so close, they're probably sitting on the floor with their backs against the door.

"Sorry. Can't. We're already asleep." My very much awake younger sister giggles. I can picture Mandy batting her eyelashes, and I can still hear her laughing.

"There's another open bed just down the hall. In Jordan's room," Mads unhelpfully adds.

"I seriously hate you." I seethe.

"No, you don't."

"You can thank us later." Their sing-song voices float through the tiny gap under the wood panel.

I groan and wipe my sweaty palms on my pajama bottoms. I know it's fruitless to argue when they're determined to force me and Jordan together. Not wanting to wake up my parents, I have two choices. I can try to sleep in one of the recliners or rocking chairs in the living room, or I can ask Jordan if I can bunk with him. And I do mean literally bunk with him, on Mike's old bunk bed. Every adult woman's dream situation: sleeping in the same room with a guy for the first time in your brother's childhood bedroom. Fabulous. Exactly what I need: Jordan thinking I'm already trying to push him for more than he might be ready to give, and my parents potentially overhearing every little creak of the springs from the other side of the wall their bedroom shares with Mike's.

With a sigh, I cross the hallway and rap lightly on his door. Jordan doesn't answer immediately, so I'm left standing alone in the hall, wondering if I should knock again. Just as I'm about to give up and surrender to a sleepless night on a squeaky old recliner, the door opens and an adorably confused Jordan is rubbing the sleep from his eyes. When he sees me, he smiles.

"Shelley? What's up?"

My brain almost forgets how to form words as my gaze slides down his bare chest and continues further to the noticeable bulge in his gray joggers, but I keep it together enough to say, "I'm sorry about this, but I need to ask you a favor."

Jordan tilts his head to one side, a soft sleepy smile still on his face, waiting to hear what I need.

"Can I sleep in here tonight? My sisters locked me out."

"They locked you out of your own room?" He seems amused. I'm not.

"Yes." I huff and cross my arms. "Sadly, it's not the first time, and it won't be the last. They like to gang up on me. It's a whole thing. They've always been like this. Can I sleep in here or…should I not?"

Jordan doesn't say anything else, just steps aside and makes a sweeping hand gesture to invite me in.

My brother's bedroom looks exactly like he left it. Dark wood bunk beds sit up against the far wall. A smattering of baseball trophies lines the top of the tall dresser, along with a bobble head of Cal Ripken. There's a framed black and white print of Mickey Mantle hitting a home run hanging on the opposite wall. Somehow this room always smells faintly of socks.

"Here, you can be on the bottom," Jordan suggests. When I pump my eyebrows suggestively, he laughs and shakes his head, moving to adjust the blankets. "Let me make the bed back up for you, and you can sleep here. I'll take the top."

I know I should tell him not to bother. I shouldn't inconvenience him more than I already am. I could climb the ladder just as well as he can. But I like the idea of snuggling into the warm spot he just vacated. And suddenly I have an aching need to breathe in the smell of that pillow.

"Thank you." I stand awkwardly with my arms swinging at my sides as he tries to straighten the quilt. "I'm sorry I woke you up."

"No worries," he assures me. "I never sleep well in new places anyway. And I was sort of hoping you'd stop by." He stops fooling with the linens long enough to exchange a heated glance with me, but he cuts it short and goes right back to his task. Interesting.

When he's satisfied enough with my new blanket arrangement, I crawl into the warm sheets, which now smell like him.

"Goodnight." He tucks the blankets around me and strokes my cheek lightly before hoisting himself onto the top bunk.

It can't possibly be comfortable for him up there. My own feet are brushing against the footboard. I'm tall at five foot ten, but Jordan is still six inches taller. He must be twisting himself into a pretzel to fit on that bed.

I lie silently for what seems like forever, flat on my back and staring up at the slats. Eventually, I blow out a breath and shift to my side, the old wood moaning as I move.

"Can't sleep?" His deep voice floats down to me and I can feel it resonate in my chest.

"Guess not." I shift again and try to find a more comfortable position, to no avail.

"I'd offer to sing a lullaby, but trust me, neither one of us wants that to happen."

"Oh, I know. I saw a video of a certain someone doing karaoke last Valentine's Day," I tease.

Jordan laughs.

"What do you do when you can't drift off?" I ask.

He chuckles again, quietly. "Have you tried snuggling Mr. Fluffers? Is he here?"

"Unfortunately, my sisters are currently holding him hostage, along with everything else in my room." I lift my leg and poke my toe into his mattress. "I'm being serious. Is there anything that helps you?"

There's a long pause, but after the beat of silence, he says, "I don't think I should answer that."

My curiosity is piqued. "No? Why is that?"

"Your innocent ears might not be ready to hear the answer," he quips.

I roll my eyes. "I know people jerk off, Jordan. You don't have to sugarcoat it. I was just hoping for a more useful answer. You know, something that might actually work for me, too."

I hear him shift above me and his tone sobers. "That still isn't working for you? I thought you said the cream was helping."

It's the first time he's the one to bring up my biggest insecurity, and it's sweet that he honestly seems concerned about me rather than wanting all the sordid details of my quest to find the ever-elusive O.

"Not yet." I sigh.

"Have you been practicing a lot?" I can hear the genuine curiosity in his question.

"Maybe." He doesn't push any further, but I offer, "I did some research, and it said audio porn worked for a lot of women better than the visual stuff. So, I paid for a month of access to a site that Mandy recommended."

"And?"

I shrug even though he can't see me. "It was a lot more comfortable for me than trying to watch the visual stuff," I admit. "But all I could think was that I knew the scenarios weren't real. I don't know those people, and they don't care about me either."

There's a long pause, and I wonder if Jordan fell asleep, but his voice is quiet and strained when he speaks again. "Do you think it would help to try with…someone who does care about you?"

Would it help?

Or would it make our entire situation infinitely more complicated than it already is?

I want to tell him about the crush I've been harboring for years, which has only grown since I accidentally sent that voice message. I want to tell him about the way my stomach squeezes and my palms get sweaty every time I see his name pop up on my phone screen, and how for the first time in my life, I actually like feeling those things. I want to tell him that being near him makes me more comfortable in my own skin, and I feel empty when he's not next to me. How I haven't been able to stop thinking about our kisses. But all those thoughts are coming too fast, one on top of the other, and I know I'll never be able to get them out the way I want to, the way he deserves to hear. So instead, I gather my courage, determined to show him.

I blink up at the wooden slats and suck in a shaky breath, knowing his body is stretched out only inches above them. "Maybe?"

"Do you, um, do you want me to try to walk you through it?"

He's trying to help you manage a medical condition, I remind myself. Plus, after what he's confided in me about his own sexuality, I know it's possible that even if he does want me, it might not be to the same degree I want him.

But I do want him.

And he *did* kiss me. Thrice.

So, I ask, "Can you come down here?"

It only takes a few seconds before he's sliding into the bottom bunk with me. I pull up the covers so he can get under them, and we lie facing each other, our bodies pressed close in the limited space of the twin bed.

I want to be clear with him. "I don't want you to do anything you don't want to do. If this is too much, you can tell me."

Jordan shakes his head. "If you think for one second that I don't want to do this, then you are severely misreading the situation." He scoots forward until there is only a breath of space between us, and his hand comes up to cup the back of my head. His fingers grasp my hair as he leans his face into mine.

"I thought…" I pause to gather the courage to tell him, "I thought maybe you didn't feel it. At least not as much as I do."

Jordan's skin brushes mine as he shakes his head. "That's not how it works. Or maybe for some people it is, I don't know." He straightens and shrugs, then his eyes lock on mine. "For me, it's more like…Well, have you ever seen Shrek?"

"Yeah?" I have no idea where he could be going with this.

"Okay, so you know how Shrek met Fiona when she was all conventionally attractive, but he really fell for her after she showed him her true form?"

"Sure." I nod along.

"That's kind of how it is for me."

"You like me now because you've seen me be ugly?"

He laughs softly. "I doubt you could ever be ugly, no matter how hard you tried. But sort of. I like you because you let me know you. The real you. The messy, chaotic, disorganized cyclone who somehow loses one sock."

I look down at my feet poking through the covers, where sure enough, one of my fuzzy socks has disappeared and the magenta polish is chipping on my uncovered toes.

Jordan is still smiling when he says, "No one has ever gotten into my head the way you have. And *that's* why I want you."

It's my turn to smile at him. "Really?" When he nods, I tell him, "That's good. Because you're in my head, too."

"Yeah?"

"Yeah." I swallow around the lump in my throat.

He brushes a kiss lightly over my eyebrow, and I bring my hand to his chest and lay it flat against his skin.

He tilts his head, and his own brow furrows. "Tell me what you're thinking, Shelley. Your body language seems like you want to be touched, but your eyes are telling me something different."

"I'm trying to figure out where to start. I don't want to make you uncomfortable or push too far for you. Can I kiss you?"

One corner of his mouth turns up in a small smirk. "Kissing is definitely an option."

"Okay. Then I choose that." I beam up at him before he leans in to brush his lips over mine. A spark ignites inside my chest, and my hands slide to his shoulders to pull him closer. He tastes like toothpaste and smells like home as my fingers slowly move up to the back of his neck so I can lock him into this moment with me.

Chapter 22

Jordan

I've lost my damn mind. I'm in Mike's room—literally in his bed—making out with his sister after I offered to help her get herself off. I'm a terrible friend, but I'm ready to accept that fact about myself because Shelley's slowly taking over every thought in my head. Her breathing has changed, and her shallow, needy sighs erase all sense of logic and reason from my brain.

When she presses her hips into me, I want to peel off every layer of fabric between us, but instead I say, "Do you still want me to try to help?"

She whimpers and nods.

"Lie back. Put two fingers in your mouth and suck on them for me."

She mumbles something to herself that sounds like "here goes nothing," but then she shifts her body and brings her fingers up, and the soft suction coming from her side of the bed is the only sound in the room.

Shelley removes her fingers and speaks again. "Now what?" she asks, tentatively, waiting for me.

I ignore the ache in my own body while I focus on telling her what to do. "Slide your hand down your body. Slowly. Stop when you get to your waistband."

Her hands are under the blankets, but I know she's doing what I tell her because her breath is uneven now. "Take your other hand and slip it under your shirt." My voice is a scratchy whisper.

"Are you hard?" she pants, but there's a hint of worry in her voice, like she's afraid my body won't react to this.

"Do you want to feel?" It's a confirmation as much as it is an invitation. I'm not planning to do anything about my own situation right now.

"Can I?"

I swallow and nod. I know we're entering new territory, and there's no coming back once we cross this line. But I shift my body and offer it to her. She seems cozy under the blanket, so I leave it draped over us, letting her set the boundaries here.

"Jordan?" Shelley hesitates and I run a finger lightly across her arm, wanting her to know I'm right here in this with her. "I need you to know I want this. So badly." She runs her teeth over her bottom lip. "But I can't promise my body will cooperate."

I put a finger to her lips to stop her before she starts an apology. I don't need her to be sorry for something she can't control.

"It feels like you're waiting for permission to be imperfect, and I should tell you you're not going to find it here," I warn her gently. "First of all, you don't need it. You're human, so be human with me," I encourage her, and she gifts me a shy smile, so I continue. "But also, I promised you I'd be honest, so I can't agree with the premise you're setting up here, because I do happen to think I'm looking at someone who's pretty damn near perfect."

"Jordan." She breathes out my name again, and it ignites a flame at the base of my spine. When our bodies are so close that barely a millimeter of space exists between us, she brings her hand out from the covers and gently runs her fingertips over my chest again. I can smell the arousal on her skin. My forehead dips down to touch hers as her other hand gently traces over my pajama bottoms. She whispers my name one last time before my lips finally land on hers.

Time and space cease to exist. There is only us here now with each other. Shelley explores my mouth with an eager curiosity while I pull her closer and let her wandering hands feel what she does to me.

Eventually, our lips part so we can each take a breath, then they briefly meet again. Two more soft, gentle kisses shared between us. A thank you and a promise. How can so much history and so many unspoken words about the future fit into one brush of her lips?

"Can I touch you, too?" I don't want to assume anything.

She offers a shaky nod. "Please."

"I'm going to try something, okay?" I wait for her permission, and when she gives it, I pull her shirt up, but not all the way off, leaving only her eyes covered, but her chest and her mouth exposed. I kiss her lips softly, then take both of her wrists gently in one of my hands and hold them against the headboard. Starting at her neck, I work my way down kissing, sucking, and nipping at her exposed skin until I reach her breasts. Licking one nipple, I blow on it gently while I lightly pinch the other between my thumb and forefinger. Her hips buck underneath me, and when I start to suck a little harder, she kicks the blanket away.

"Do you like that?"

She whimpers again, and the fabric of her shirt bunches around her head as she nods.

"Good. Let me see how much." I alternate sucking, nibbling, and blowing on her while my right hand travels down to the waistband of her shorts. I run one finger along the top, and she whines. I chuckle and whisper, "Patience, Sweetheart. I know it's hard, but I need you to be quiet."

Her knees fall open in a silent plea for more. Moving at an agonizingly slow pace, I lower my hand to the bottom hem of her shorts and pull the fabric to the side, stroking over the wet spot that's forming on her underwear.

"What do you want, Shelley?" I continue rubbing over the fabric while I let go of her wrists. She leaves her hands where I had them.

"Touch me. Please," she begs, her eyes still covered.

"I can do that, but only if you promise to hold still and be quiet. Do you think you can do that for me?" I ask, peeling her sleep shorts and her underwear down her legs and discarding them at the foot of the bed.

"Yes."

"Good girl. I'm going to make sure the door is locked, and I'm going to turn on some music. Then I'm going to come back and spend a long time right here." I drag one finger over her dripping crease before moving to do exactly what I promised. I double-check the lock and set a playlist on my phone to low volume. I don't want to wake anyone, but I do want to keep them from overhearing. The noises she's making tonight are for my ears only.

I return to the bed quickly and turn her body so she's sideways on the mattress. Dropping to my knees on the floor in front of her, I drape her legs over my shoulders. I bring her hands down and set them on her belly while I fully uncover her face and look into her eyes. "If you want me to stop, you can say so, or just tap on my head. I'll stop right away, I promise. But I don't think you're going to want me to." I wink at her.

Those stormy gray irises staring back at me hold my entire future. It should be terrifying, but instead it just feels right. Like this is exactly where I belong.

Chapter 23

Shelley

The makeshift blindfold and the music on Jordan's playlist have helped to calm the chaos in my brain, so now I can concentrate on the way he's touching me. It only takes three songs before a slow heat spreads through my body, and I think I'm about to shatter on his tongue. But then the building release fades into nothing.

I'm so frustrated with myself I think I might start to cry.

Sensing the shift in me, Jordan sits back on his heels. "You okay?"

"I'm so sorry. I was almost there," I explain. "I know this is taking forever. You don't have to keep going."

Jordan rises to meet me, holding himself in a push-up position over my body while he growls low in my ear. "Stop apologizing. We're in the middle of the best night of my life. I'm exactly where I want to be, and I'll stay on my knees for you for as long as you let me. Do you still feel good?"

"Yes," I admit.

"Do you want me to stop?"

"No."

"Then I'm not stopping."

And he doesn't. Twice more the gentle wave starts to crest before disappearing into nothing. Finally, I resign to accept that there is no finish line and I can sink into the enjoyment of his touch.

That's when it hits me out of nowhere. Every muscle tenses, right down to my toes, and I gasp loudly.

The groan that comes out of him as he laps up my release is the hottest sound I've ever heard. I laugh as a tear of relief slides down my cheek.

My body actually responded. I'm in shock. "Oh my god. You did it. *I* did it. We did it. I wasn't sure that could happen." I pant, barely recognizing the sense of awe and wonder in my own voice. Jordan wipes my tear away with one finger. "That was amazing," I tell him. "Thank you. I'm so happy. And you—"

"Are still not finished."

He's insatiable. Jordan kept me awake almost the entire night, not that I'm complaining. We didn't make it past third base, but I'll never forget the things he whispered while he made me come once more with his fingers. Then he let me use my hands on him.

We drifted off briefly, snuggled together on the cramped bottom bed, and woke up this morning with sore necks and backs. Totally worth it. And for the record, I was right. After spending last night in his arms, I'm completely gone for him.

We had an early plane to catch, so both of us slept during the whole flight back to D.C. We're finally starting to look a little less like zombies, or at least that's what I'm telling myself, by the time we deboard the plane and make our way out to the gate.

"I'm starving," Jordan complains from behind me as he drags a rolling suitcase in each hand because he insists on carrying mine along with his own.

I flick the brim of his backwards cap and tease, "You poor thing. Did I not feed you well enough last night?"

"Oh, you definitely did. I'm never washing this beard again. It was like a baptism."

"Gross." But he has me laughing. "There's a Wing Pit around the corner here." I point, directing him toward one of my favorite casual dining options, but I stop short because of the commotion. An entire film crew is posted outside the restaurant. But it still appears to be open and seating other patrons, so we continue, dodging the cameras. Then I see her. "Oh my god. That's Stacy Haverson!"

I freeze, barely remembering to breathe. It feels like all the wind has been knocked out of me. She's here. In the flesh. Barely ten feet away, with a face covered in wing sauce as they film what must be an upcoming social media challenge, according to the huge hashtag posters displayed behind her.

"What's going on?" Jordan comes to a halt just before bumping into me.

I can't answer because I'm completely fixated on watching my favorite athlete demolish the two buckets of wings set out in front of her, but I do notice when Jordan takes a step back.

"This line is insane. It's going to be a while before it dies down. I'm going to go grab a sub from over there," he offers, pointing across the terminal. "You want one?"

I nod at him, only half paying attention, and turn back to watching Stacy. She seems to be finished at least one bucket of wings already. Jordan leaves my suitcase by my side and heads toward the Sub Shack. Pulling out my phone, I quickly snap a photo to send to the sisters group chat before I check Stacy's social media feed.

It turns out, the challenge is to eat one hundred chicken wings and a large side of curly fries in under an hour, and she finishes at the forty-seven-minute mark. The small crowd claps, and most people disperse to go about the rest of their day. Stacy excuses herself to the restroom to wash her hands, and I stay behind to see if she'd be willing to take a selfie or sign the tank top I've pulled out of my suitcase.

As I'm waiting, Jordan returns.

"There you are," I say. "Do you want to split some wings now that it's not so busy?"

"Nah, it's okay." He shakes his head, holding up his sandwich. "I got you buffalo chicken, since that seems to be the theme today."

I thank him and tell him I'd like to stay to meet Stacy, if she's available.

"Sure. Do you want me to go with you?"

"If you want to."

He chuckles. "You want to have your fangirl moment alone, don't you?" When I don't argue, he says, "It's cool. I'll just be waiting over there." He points at the airport lounge chairs sitting further down the corridor.

"Okay. Thank you." I nod at him and make my way over to the short line of people now waiting. Stacy graciously takes her time with everyone who wants to say hi, but it only takes a few minutes until my turn comes.

"Hi, I'm Michelle Miller. You can call me Shelley. That was amazing! I've been watching you online for years, but seeing it in person was something else," I gush at her.

She smiles politely, one hand resting on her very full and now protruding belly. "Nice to meet you, Shelley. Thank you so much for following my journey. Are you a competitive eater, too?"

"Oh, no. Just a big fan. Do you think you could sign my shirt, please?"

Her face lights up when I hand it over. "Oh my gosh, you really are an O.G. fan, aren't you? This is from my very first line of merch."

I nod. "I know. I think you only had about three hundred followers when I subscribed to your channel." She's up to almost a million now. Stacy happily signs my shirt, and we pose for a photo, which she asks for permission to share on her own social channels.

I'm beaming as we say goodbye and I return to the chairs where Jordan is waiting.

"She was so nice," I tell him.

He smiles and stands to collect his luggage before handing me a plastic bag with my sub in it. "That's awesome. I'm glad you got to meet her."

Before everything that happened yesterday, I would have thought meeting Stacy would be the highlight of this trip. But now this memory has some intense competition. Maybe Jordan wasn't exaggerating when he said last night was the best one of his life. I think I know how he feels.

"So…I guess this is goodbye for now?" I'm disappointed it's time to part ways, but I won't dwell on it too much because I'm still riding the high of meeting my favorite celebrity. Besides, it won't be long before I see Jordan again. By this time next week, we're going to be neighbors.

"For now." He moves in close, threading his fingers through my hair while I look up at him. "But we'll still have the phone. That's what started all of this, after all."

"I guess I'm better at leaving voicemails than I thought," I tease.

"I won't argue with that. I'm looking forward to talking to you tonight." His lips graze my ear as he whispers. "You can tell me what you liked about last night, and what you want to try next time."

I manage to contain the shiver his words send through me. "I could probably fill a book with that information."

He laughs. "Yeah?"

"Well, at least a long email," I say, wrapping my arms around his neck.

"Oh, I'm definitely going to hold you to that. I *really* want to see this email."

"I can do that. But only if you write one, too."

"Deal." He squeezes me in an intimate hug.

"Then I guess you better let me go home and start typing," I say, poking his side as he releases me.

He nods, and his hands rest on my hips as he leans in again. Our goodbye kiss feels more like a new beginning.

Chapter 24

Shelley

Jordan: I'm going to have to mark this assignment incomplete. None of these are fantasies. This is a tiny list of the three most basic positions known to humans.

My cheeks heat as I read Jordan's text. He read my email then. Missing him and feeling bold last night, I decided to follow through with his suggestion to send my fantasies. I thought it would be sexy, but now it feels a little humiliating.

Me: Maybe I misunderstood? Apparently, I'm not a good student.

Jordan: Sorry, Law School, I'm not buying that one at all.

Me: Ugh. I need an example, then. What exactly are you looking for with this "assignment?" And you didn't even send yours yet. Why am I the only one being vulnerable?

Jordan: I didn't realize you were really going to do it so quickly. I thought I still had a few days. But fair enough. You write out a more detailed scene, and I'll write one, too. Try to be specific. We'll send them to each other by midnight. Deal?

Midnight tonight? Six hours from now, I could have a detailed description of Jordan's fantasies in my inbox? I let him sweat it out a few minutes before responding.

Me: *Those terms are agreeable.*

Jordan: *It's hot when you put on your courtroom voice, Counselor.*

I'm still smiling while I send an eyeroll emoji.

Me: *Save the role play for your scene. Get to writing.*

Jordan: *Yes, ma'am.*

Turning to my computer, I start typing. Midnight can't come fast enough. The words fly out of me, and it doesn't take me long to finish my story and hit send.

At eleven-forty-two, I get his email. Not that I've been obsessively checking, and not that I set notifications and a specific sound alert for everything that comes through from his account or anything.

I think it would be cool to come home to someone wearing my jersey, and nothing else. Maybe we eat a meal or play a game. Then they sit on my lap and things get heated.

Three sentences? His fantasy email contains exactly three sentences, and they aren't even long ones. I, on the other hand, wrote a two-thousand-word short story. He's going to think I'm too much. That is, if he even responds at all. What if I scare him off with my over-eager intensity? I must admit, I do like the idea of wearing his jersey and sitting on his lap, though.

My phone buzzes with a new text.

Jordan: *Are you awake? Is it okay to call?*

I send a thumbs up and a smiley face, and only a few seconds pass before my phone rings. Neither of us bothers to say hello.

"Wow. That was…descriptive," he says.

"I'm so embarrassed. I thought you wanted me to go into detail?"

"I'm glad you did. I think I learned some things about myself from reading this." He laughs, and that warm feeling floods my chest again and eases my nerves. Talking to Jordan feels like sipping on spiced apple cider while I sit by a fire, wrapped in my favorite blanket. He's warm, and cozy, and familiar. Fun, but in a safe, comfortable way. Which is my favorite kind of fun.

"I think you officially know more about me than anyone else ever has," I tell him, truthfully.

"I'm honored."

There's a long beat of silence, but it isn't unwelcome. I assume we're both thinking about my email. I know I am.

A big part of me regrets getting so specific, but an even bigger part is secretly thrilled with the idea that Jordan read those thoughts, and he wasn't turned off. He's still here. I haven't scared him away. If anything, he seems accepting. Maybe even a little bit intrigued.

"Are you going to tell me what you learned?" I ask, coyly. There's no point in holding back now. It's open flirting season.

He hums into the phone, and I can practically feel the low vibration caress my skin. "I like the way you started your story at the beginning of a date, like you saw everything leading up to the physical stuff as foreplay."

I'm not prepared for the way my whole body reacts when he says that word.

"Maybe you should read me your favorite parts." Who even am I right now?

I don't know, but Jordan seems to like this version of me because he chuckles and says, "Yeah? I can do that. But only if we get on a video call because I want to see your cheeks get all red when you get hot and bothered by your own words."

On cue, I feel my face heat. It won't be my words turning me on, it will be his voice reading them, but either way. "Deal."

As soon as I hang up, a new video call from him comes through. My face is way too close to the camera, and the shaky video quality leaves much to be desired. On Jordan's end, I can see his whole torso, and he's sitting still in the center of the frame, with a paper in his hand.

"Did you actually print it out?" I'm as impressed as I am horrified by that idea. "And do you have your phone on a tripod? Why do you own a tripod? Do you do these kinds of calls a lot?" A sharp pang of jealousy hits. I *really* don't like the idea of anyone else getting to be on a call like this with Jordan.

He waits patiently for me to finish my mini-interrogation before he answers. "My phone is propped up against a stack of books on a chair. But no more changing the subject. We're here to discuss this brilliant piece." He clears his throat and grabs a pair of reading glasses from the nightstand.

With his beard and now the glasses, he's got a whole hot, nerdy professor vibe going on, and it's really working for me. When he starts to read, I hide my face behind my hands, peeking at him through the cracks in my fingers. He looks straight into the camera and smiles. "No hiding now, Sea Shell. You wrote this." He waves the papers in his hand. "You're going to own it."

A huge cheesy grin spreads across my face at his use of my silly nickname. Even though I'm feeling slightly nauseated by the idea that Jordan Wagner is about to read my own spicy email back to me, I am undeniably excited at the prospect.

"I took the liberty of highlighting a few parts."

"You did not."

He raises his eyebrows and turns the paper toward the camera so I can see it. Sure enough, there are several lines marked with neon yellow ink. "I'm very studious when I want to be." That smirk on his lips does delicious things to me.

His eyes return to the paper as he reads, "*After a light dinner, where we both avoid gassy foods or anything that will give us bad breath and eat something light and safe, like turkey wraps...* Practical. Okay, I'm with you. *We'll do something fun like ice-skating or an arcade. Then we'll go to a neutral location, maybe a bougie hotel. That way I don't have to invite him to my place, but I also don't have to worry about if he washed his sheets recently.* I'm down for an arcade. Making a note to wash my sheets as soon as we hang up."

I scrunch my nose, but I laugh. He reads through the rest of my email, stopping to discuss every minute detail and ask me questions as he stares into my soul with that intense eye contact of his, as if he truly is studying my response.

"The smell thing is really important to you, huh?"

"Is it not to you?"

"Honestly, I've never really thought about it. But I guess not. I'd still want you if your breath smelled like garlic."

"Ew. Why?"

His voice is tender when he says, "Because you're you." Then he continues reading. *"He has a playlist of instrumental music because lyrics in songs can be really distracting to me. See? These are the things I need to know."* Jordan smiles and says, "I highlighted this next part. Ahem. *When we get going, I'm on all fours and he touches me from behind, maybe while I use a toy on myself, too."*

Yep, he was correct. My face must be a thousand degrees. I bring my hands up to cover my eyes, but Jordan tisks at me. "Uh-uh, no hiding. This is a masterpiece."

"It may have been inspired by recent events," I admit, lowering my hands.

"I was hoping you'd say that. Now, where was I?"

I never want this call to end, but eventually exhaustion hits and we're both yawning and nodding off. As much as I would rather stay up with him all night, there's been a lot of that lately, and my body is begging for sleep.

"Goodnight, Jordan."

"Night, Sea Shell. Sweet dreams."

There's no doubt in my mind they will be now.

Chapter 25

Jordan

Miller didn't even question it when I offered to tag along for Shelley's move since he was glad for the help. It's the end of the semester and most students have already gone home, so there's more parking in front of the building than the last time I was here, and it doesn't take us long to find a spot.

Shelley greets us at the door once we make it up to her unit.

"Thank you so much for this. You're both total lifesavers. Whatever you want, it's yours. My first-born child? My rainbow unicorn sticker book from the third grade? You name it."

"It's deeply concerning to hear you value those two things equally." Mike gives her a quick hug, then walks past his sister and starts scanning the space, assessing the job we have ahead of us today.

"In my defense, they were great stickers. Holographic. Easy to peel but stayed where you put them." Shelley's eyes soften when she turns her focus to me. "Hi."

"Hi."

We're frozen, all deep stares and wide smiles until Mike twists his face at our strange behavior. "Can we get started or what? I don't want to be here all day."

"Right." I clap my hands in front of me, scanning the half-packed boxes and open trash bags stuffed with clothes. "What can we do first?"

"I could use your help with some stuff in my room." She winks, and I widen my eyes at her.

"Your brother is *right there. Behave.*" My whisper is barely audible. I glance at Mike, but he's already headed toward the open front door with an armful of stacked boxes.

Shelley ignores him as she leads me to her bedroom. "Right this way."

When we hear Mike's footsteps fade down the hall, she closes the door and jumps onto me, wrapping her arms around my neck and her legs around my waist.

Surprised, I catch her and say, "You're going to get us in trouble if you can't control yourself today."

"Uh-oh, what are you going to do? Spank me?" Her face beams as she teases.

Okay, maybe I'm the one who's in trouble here, but I smirk at her and nuzzle my beard into her neck, the way I've learned she likes. "Maybe later, if you're lucky, but right now you get one kiss. One. Then we're going to be on our best behavior and do nothing but move boxes until we're alone tonight in North Bay. Got it?"

"Okay, Party Pooper. Guess I better make this one count if it needs to last all day." She kisses me deeply, but we both know we can't do this for long if we're going to maintain our cover around her brother. Reluctantly, she climbs down and lets me go, but not before squeezing me tightly. I hug her back, burying my face in her hair and relishing the brief moment of comfort.

The door handle jostles, and we jump apart just as Mike comes into the room. "Got any more packing tape? I was halfway down the steps when the bottom of a box fell out. Don't worry, nothing broke. It was just clothes."

"Oh, um…" Shelley smooths her shirt as she gathers her thoughts. "I think I might've put it in one of the boxes."

"You packed the packing tape?" He groans, incredulous.

"Don't give her a hard time," I interject. "Moving can be stressful. I'm sure we can find more tape."

"Thank you, Jordan." Shelley smiles, inching closer until we're next to each other.

Mike rolls his eyes at me. "Can you stop kissing my sister's ass for just a minute and give me a hand out there, please? Her stuff is still scattered all over the hall." What would he do if he knew I've already kissed so much more than that?

"Yeah, I'm coming."

Since the furniture in her apartment is owned by the school, there is less to move than we expected. Mike tackles most of the boxes, only needing me when he can't manage to move two huge containers of hardback books and binders by himself. I'm sure those books are stuffed full of legal jargon I couldn't pronounce if my life depended on it. The heavy buggers are an unwelcome reminder of exactly how out of my league this woman is, and the dull ache in my elbow is an unpleasant reminder about why my career is coming to an end. I try not to dwell on either of those facts as we toss the remaining trash bags and laundry baskets filled with clothes and blankets into the back of the truck. We cover all of it with a tarp so none of it ends up scattered on the highway.

Shelley rides between us on the bench seat, subtly pressing her thigh into mine the whole ride home until we pull into the parking lot of our complex. It takes less time to unload the boxes and carry them upstairs than it did to pack them, but by the time we've gotten all her things into her new apartment, which is only five doors down the hall from mine, we're all ready to crash. At least this place was furnished, too, so we didn't have to lug a couch up three flights of stairs.

This apartment is a mirror image of my own, except hers only has one bedroom. Otherwise, the open kitchen and living room look exactly the same, and the small hallway leads to her bedroom and bathroom.

Mike and I take a seat on her new furniture, and Shelley hands us each a bottle of water. She fans herself with one hand, her face splotchy from exertion. It conjures images of my favorite night in recent memory.

She groans. "Ugh. Not looking forward to doing that all over again in a few months. Maybe I should call your friend in the fall. What's his name? Davis? Isn't this what he does now?"

I huff out a small laugh. "Sort of the opposite. He throws things away for people. But if you call him in the fall, I'll probably be the one answering anyway."

"What does that mean?" Mike asks, setting down his water. He and Shelley both look at me with the same concerned gray eyes and questioning crease on their foreheads. Might as well tell them.

"I'm retiring after this season. I talked to Coach this week. Davis offered me a job." I shrug, downplaying it. We're all tired, and I don't want to make this a big deal.

"Really? You sure?" Mike leans forward. When I nod, he clasps a hand on my shoulder and says, "I know the team will miss you."

"You're staying in North Bay, though?" Shelley confirms.

I nod at her, too. "It feels like home here," I admit. The friends I've made in this town feel more like family than my actual blood. I don't want to leave. I know Mike understands. He made the same choice to put down roots here.

He blows out a breath, "Wow. That's a big change. Glad you're sticking around. On or off the field, this town needs you."

"Thanks, man."

Then he turns his attention to his sister. "You good for the night, Shell? I have to head out. I'm on a flight to Seattle in the morning." His eyes meet mine, sending a silent bro code signal to watch out for her. I nod at him one more time.

"I'm a big girl, I'll be fine," Shelley assures her brother. She thanks him for the help, and they say their goodbyes. As soon as the door closes behind him, she turns to me. "I seem to remember hearing something about a spanking."

I shake my head. "Let me feed you first, you little horndog. Do you want some pizza? There's a place in Marnock, the next town over, that delivers out this way."

"That sounds great, but you are absolutely not buying this time. I forbid it."

"Is that so?" I pull her onto my lap and tickle her ribs until she's squealing and squirming. Little does she know, I have no plans to ever let her get away.

Chapter 26

Shelley

Since next year I'll need to do my internship and gain work experience, this is probably the last official summer break I'll have until I'm old enough to retire. And my new sister-in-law is insisting we use it to attend morning yoga.

If North Bay is going to be my home for the next few months, I want to make an effort to fit in with Danielle and her friends. So, even though I could be taking a rare opportunity to sleep in, I dutifully report to the parking lot of my apartment building at eight-thirty, wearing my leggings and a sports bra covered by a loose tank.

Danielle is already waiting. "You look amazing!" She cheerily starts a conversation as she bounces up to me. There's a canvas tote bag on her arm and a metal water bottle in her hand. "Alice texted. She's checking on something at the studio, but she'll meet us over there. Regina said she might join us and bring her daughter, Emily."

I groan, digging through my purse to produce my sunglasses, then sliding them on to protect myself from the brutal assault of early morning light. "Too early. Too many words. Not enough caffeine."

"Not a morning person, I take it?"

"Didn't get a lot of sleep," I admit.

After we demolished a large pizza, Jordan insisted on staying late last night to help me unpack my boxes. By the time he went back to his apartment, I was still buzzing with energy from the way his presence jolts every cell in my body to attention. I couldn't sleep, so I stayed awake reliving our first night together, the video call where he read my email, then last night...

Danielle's voice pulls me out of my daydream. "Oh? Mike said when he left yesterday Jordan was going to stay and help you unpack. Were you two working late?" she asks as she walks me to her book van.

"Um, yeah. I guess we lost track of time." My eyes slide over to gauge if she read anything into that statement, but she only adjusts the radio dial and continues making small talk as we head into town.

Downtown North Bay consists of exactly one street. It's a tiny waterfront peninsula which boasts almost every business in this town. Most of the storefronts do double-duty, like Brew-Ha-Ha, the coffee house/comedy club/karaoke bar. We park outside a building with vinyl letters on the window that read, "Fringe. Hair & Yoga." I shake my head and follow as Danielle leads us inside. The bottom floor is a beauty salon with three adjustable chairs situated in front of mirrors. We go up a set of wooden stairs to the yoga space, which I've been informed also doubles as a meeting room for Honey's spicy book club twice a month, and we spread our mats on the floor. It isn't long before some familiar faces join us, along with a few more people I don't know.

Our instructor is a tall woman with wild, red hair and a jade necklace. She introduces herself as "Samantha around town, but here in our shared space, please call me Anthem." She greets us each individually with a tiny bow before she presses play on an old boom box, which sits atop a wooden stool in the corner. The sound of an acoustic guitar drifts into the air, but the music is so low it almost feels like I need to close my eyes to hear it.

Anthem invites us to borrow pillows, bolsters, and blankets from her stash and demonstrates our first position. I've taken yoga classes before at my gym back home, but this one is different. She explains, probably for my benefit as the only newbie, that this is a restorative yoga class that focuses on gentle stretching, relaxation, and stress relief.

"That sounds like exactly what I need," I whisper to Danielle before I tuck a bolster pillow at the end of my mat. As reluctant as I was to come this morning, I find I'm really enjoying myself. I don't usually have a chance to focus on nothing but relaxation. Law school is a lot of things, but a chill environment is not one of them. The yoga class ends up being a welcome break. I think I even fell asleep for a little while when we were doing Savasana. I didn't realize how much I've been craving girl time without having my sisters nearby, and Alice and Danielle seem happy to stand in. Emily is adorable trying to hold her balance in tree pose.

When the class is over, I'm so relaxed I feel slightly hungover. I will definitely need to find a yoga studio when I return to D.C. Alice quickly excuses herself to head back to Just Art. It's cute that she and Jake thought they were hiding their feelings for each other for so long when it's obvious she can't stand being away from him for more than an hour at a time. I wonder if she can tell Jordan and I are doing the same thing now?

After we wave goodbye to her friends, Danielle turns to me. "Should the two of us do a sisters' brunch over at Brew-Ha-Ha? They have the raspberry white chocolate scones on Mondays. And I feel like I never get to see you while you're at school. I know it's old hat to you, but I've never had a sister before, and I'm excited!"

"Welcome to the club. My treat, since you're driving me around today." Unlike Jordan, Danielle takes me up on the offer immediately.

We head over to the coffee shop and I buy a chai latte and a scone for each of us, then we sit down to catch up. I make a mental note to ask for a job application before we leave. Maybe I could get a summer job here and start paying down some of my loans. Danielle tells me about the challenges of building her new book delivery business, and how tough it's been to share Mike's time with the new team, and I offer a few stories about school. I want to tell her what's going on with Jordan, but there's no way to guarantee she won't take the information back to my brother.

When a new text from Jordan comes through, I can't stop myself from looking.

Danielle's eyes scan my face, then she points to my phone. "Is that a guy, perhaps?"

"It's nothing." I shrug and try to play it cool, but her knowing nod tells me she's forming her own theories.

"Doesn't look like nothing to me. That's an *I like him* face."

Danielle and Alice are the only people in this town I could talk to about what's happening, but Alice isn't here, and I don't want to ask Danielle to hide this from her husband.

"Okay, fine. But it's just a little crush."

She leans in, setting her elbows on the table and resting her chin on her hand. "Oooh, care to share?"

I shake my head and raise my cup to take a long sip. "Never mind me. Tell me about married life."

"I know you know this, but Mike's so great," she gushes, launching into a story about how he put out a small kitchen fire when Honey got distracted gossiping on the phone with her friend Edna and left an oven mitt too close to an open flame.

"Wow. Yeah. Good thing he was there," I agree.

"I know, right? I don't know what I would do without him."

Even when he's not here, I can always count on my brother to suck up all the attention in a room. This time I'm grateful for it.

Chapter 27

Shelley

"Is Jake eating with us?" I ask. Jake's old bulldog, Hazel, is lounging on her bed in the corner. She raises her head when she hears her owner's name, but then she flops right back down again. Jordan invited me over for dinner. He's making a huge bowl of Greek salad, which will be topped with grilled chicken.

"Nah. He offered to drive Alice's dad to an appointment. Mr. Caulfield had some health issues recently. Jake's been helping their family. We've got the place to ourselves." Jordan wags his eyebrows, causing me to laugh.

"What's that for?" I point at the container of plain yogurt sitting out on the counter.

"We're making tzatziki."

"We're making it? Like, from scratch?" I eye the cucumber and lemon laid out next to the yogurt. "Okay, it's official. This is the most impressive thing I've ever seen."

He shakes his head. "That's sad. It's like five ingredients. We're not solving differential equations over here. Can you hand me that microplane?"

"If I knew what a microplane looked like, I would surely do that for you."

Jordan points to a device on the other side of the counter and I stretch to reach for it. The metal contraption looks like something the nail techs use to scrape off dead skin when my sisters take me for pedicures. I hand it over, and Jordan starts sliding a tiny piece of garlic against the metal. It smells amazing in here.

"Can you slice the chicken?" he asks, gesturing to the cutting board where the cooked meat is resting while he starts on the cucumber.

I nod and get to work cutting it into thin strips. When I'm finished, he arranges the warm meat over a big bowl of lettuce with lots of tomatoes and thinly sliced red onion. Then he explains that the Greek yogurt in the dressing we're making will add extra protein as well.

"I have no doubt it will be one of the best things I've ever eaten."

"Sounds like you have high expectations over there."

"I do. Someone taught me I needed to raise my standards. And yet you continue to meet the new bar."

He smiles before going back to watching what he's doing. My phone buzzes a few times in the back pocket of my jeans, but I ignore it while I set a bent elbow on the counter and rest my chin on my fist so I can watch Jordan work. He adds lemon juice, dill, salt, and pepper to the small bowl along with the garlic, cucumber, and yogurt.

Dipping a spoon in the sauce, he holds it out for me. "Want to taste?"

I lean forward to take it into my mouth. As my tongue curls around the metal, warmth spreads through me. It's nice to let someone take care of me. Jordan's eyes find mine as he uses his thumb to gently stroke my cheek.

"It's really good," I tell him. He smiles again, and his chest puffs up just a little bit. I move to plate some salad for each of us, and we sit together at his kitchen island to eat.

It's honestly starting to scare me how much I like this man. I've never been this into another person. But we both know this can't last. I'm only in North Bay temporarily. All the reasons we held off being together for so long are still lurking in the future, waiting for us to come down from this lover's high and make our crash landing back in reality.

"Hey, um, thanks again for helping with my move. And for taking the time to go through all those boxes with me. I know I've been creating a lot of extra work for you recently. I really appreciate it." I keep my eyes on my plate and shovel a tomato into my mouth.

Jordan sets down his fork and looks at me. "You're welcome for the move. But I've been thoroughly enjoying every second with you. Purely selfish on my end. No need to thank me," he insists, placing a hand on my thigh.

I purse my lips and tilt my head at him, because how could it not be extra work for him? It's not just the move. He spent hours learning my body when we were on that bunk bed. He's always so careful to consider my needs and make sure to give me options that feel safe.

"I know I'm a lot," I admit.

He shakes his head again, serious this time. "It makes me a little sad to know other people have made you feel that way. There's nothing wrong with having needs. You've been really patient with respecting my boundaries, too."

I scoff. "That's different."

"I don't see how."

"Because all I had to do was wait to see if you would catch feelings. But being with me puts an actual physical burden on you. I'm sure you've never been with anyone who takes as much work as I do to be with."

"And? So what if your needs are different than mine, or anyone else's for that matter?"

I blink at him and he sighs, reaching out to stroke my hair.

"Let me try to explain it another way. Let's say we were sitting together on the sofa. If I said my elbow hurt and I asked you to move so I could shift to another position, would you think twice about trying to make me more comfortable?"

"Of course not." It would be ridiculous to make him sit there in pain when I could do something as easy as scoot over a few inches. "But what does that have to do with anything?"

"Why is it any different if you're uncomfortable in bed and we need to make some adjustments?"

I blink at him. I don't have an answer. I don't know why. I only know it's been my experience that it usually bothers people when I ask them to change their routine around me. I never questioned it because, to be honest, a big part of me understood how it might be annoying when I'm the only one in a group who can't handle things. Loud music or bright lights might not be bothering someone else the way they bother me. It's not fair for me to ask a whole group of friends to leave a party early just because I've hit my limit and can't handle any more peopling. So, how could it be fair to ask even more of a romantic partner? Isn't it selfish to need people to change their plans just for me?

But I guess he has a point. I wouldn't think Jordan was being selfish or unreasonable in the example he just gave.

"Maybe it's not," I admit. "But I'm not used to it, and sometimes it's hard to accept you're being genuine because I've gotten a lot of pushback on this kind of stuff before."

"I'm sorry you went through that. But I'm not other people, Shelley." His promise glides over me like sunscreen, smooth and protective, a barrier between me and the things that could hurt.

"No. You're not."

He gives me a soft, warm smile. "If you want to stick around and watch a movie or something, that's cool. But I'm going to shower and turn in early. I'm supposed to be at the field first thing tomorrow."

Armed with the newfound confidence he's helped me gain, I decide to be direct and ask for what I want.

"Can I join you in the shower?"

I want to show him exactly how much I appreciate how patient and attentive he's been.

A low sound rumbles in his throat. "Like you need to ask."

Chapter 28

Jordan

It barely registers that Jake must be home when the front door opens and shuts in the distance. Everything I have is focused on Shelley as she kneels in front of me, water pouring down on both of us. I gather her hair and hold it in one fist. She looks up at me, droplets gathered on her eyelashes.

"Damn, Sweetheart, you look gorgeous on your knees." My breath hitches and I hiss as she flattens her tongue and glides against my sensitive skin. When she hollows her cheeks and starts to suck, I have to brace an arm on the shower wall for balance. My eyes are transfixed as her fingers trail down her body, dipping between her thighs. "Good girl. Make yourself feel good while you have your mouth around me."

A banging on the bathroom door startles us both. "Jordan? Are you home? Jake, is that you in the shower? Have you seen Jordan?" Mike's voice comes from the hall. "He's not answering my calls."

Shelley and I both freeze at the sound of her brother's question. Her eyes go wide for a second, but then she gets a mischievous glint in her eye and goes back to working me over.

"Uh, yeah. It's me in here," I call out to him, trying and failing to keep my words even. I lower my voice to whisper to Shelley, "I'm strongly rethinking my decision to let him keep his key."

"Shelley isn't answering her phone or the door at her apartment. Do you know where she is? She's not with Danielle, and she doesn't have a car. I know this sounds nuts because she just got here, but I'm getting worried she might be sneaking around with someone. What if she's in some kind of trouble?" Miller can be kind of paranoid about protecting the people he loves.

Shelley pops off of me and cups a hand over her mouth to cover her laugh.

"It's not funny," I insist, still whispering. She seems to disagree. Her shoulders are shaking because she can't stop giggling. I've kept things hidden from him, but I've never outright lied to my best friend, and I don't want to start now. But something tells me Miller doesn't actually want to know why his sister isn't answering her phone.

"You'd have to ask her, man," I call out to him. There. Not exactly a lie.

Shelley's quiet laughing fit hits so hard I think there might be tears running down her cheeks, but it's hard to tell in the shower. She accidentally knocks down a bottle of shampoo, and it falls into the tub with an echoing thud. "Oops."

"Is someone in there with you?"

"Um…"

"Oh. Sorry. My bad. I'm leaving. Just let me know if you hear from her, okay? I'm getting worried."

"I'm sure she's fine," I shout, pulling Shelley up from the shower floor and cupping my hand over her mouth. Her laughter is contagious and I'm two seconds away from losing it myself. "Not funny," I repeat, lowering my voice to scold her while I press my body into hers. Her eyes dance over the top of my fingers. She licks my hand, but I hold it there.

"And for the record, I told you you'd never make it to the end of the season before breaking that stupid celibacy vow!" Mike calls before we hear the front door shut.

"That was way too close," I say, finally letting her go.

Shelley digs her fingers into my hips, pulling me into her. "Forget him. Where were we?"

I finally let myself smile at her. "If I remember correctly, one of us was on our knees."

Her own grin spreads further, and that sultry tone is back when she raises a hand to my shoulder and says, "Hmm. Then I guess *one of us* better get back down there."

I don't fight it when she presses her fingers into my skin, I just drop down and get to work.

Chapter 29

Shelley

After my brother's little interruption, Jordan and I finish our shower. I didn't manage to come this time, but it doesn't matter. The way Jordan worships my body without expecting anything from it gives me a new appreciation for what it means to truly be in the moment with him.

When we're dry and dressed again, we head down the hall to my place, since my brother doesn't have a key to my door and Jake will be coming back to the guys' apartment soon. This way we can guarantee there will be no more surprise interruptions. I send Mikey a quick proof of life text to get him off my back before I snuggle into bed with his best friend, both of us stripping down to our bare skin again because, whether or not we fool around anymore tonight, I still crave the feeling of Jordan's skin against mine.

"I had a lot of fun with you tonight," he says.

"Mmm," I mumble as he nestles his face into my hair.

"You seem tired."

"I am." I yawn. "I think you wore me out. I'm sorry."

"It's okay. Go to sleep. I'll be right here."

It's easy to drift off with Jordan's fingers trailing barely-there strokes down my arm as he whispers gentle affirmations in my ear.

I don't know what time it is when a loud, steady beep startles me out of my reverie and the sense of calm relaxation is replaced with panic.

The smoke alarm. I guess I spoke too soon about surprise interruptions.

Jordan tosses me his t-shirt from the floor, and he pulls on a pair of sweatpants before we hurry toward the front door, both of us barefoot. As soon as my door is open, the beeping intensifies. The hallway smells terrible, but people aren't rushing, and I don't see any smoke. It seems likely to be a false alarm. Getting swept along with the crowd, we join our neighbors as we all file out of the building and into the parking lot.

I spot Jake and Alice, who seem to be back to trying to avoid each other. His head is down, and her arms are crossed as she faces away from him. Hopefully, they won't notice me and I can avoid having to answer for my current state of undress. But Jordan doesn't understand the assignment, and he calls out and waves to them. He takes my wrist and tugs me in their direction while I try to use my other hand to pull the t-shirt down far enough to cover all my assets. As soon as we're standing together, it's clear Jake and Alice are too engaged in an argument of their own to notice what I'm wearing.

"How hard is it to follow the directions? They are printed right on the bag!" Alice moves her hands to her hips while she turns and glares up at her boyfriend. They're official now.

"I thought it would be faster." Jake shrugs.

"Wait. What happened?" Jordan asks.

Alice explodes as she throws her hands up. "This guy set the microwave timer for *nine* minutes instead of the typical two it takes to make popcorn."

"It was an accident. The nine was right next to the popcorn button," Jake tries to defend himself, but it falls flat because fifty people are standing on asphalt in our pajamas because of him. "I guess I need to go take care of this," he mutters before moving to the front of the crowd and announcing, "Sorry, folks. This was all me. I apologize for the inconvenience, but I promise there's no fire. The only casualties tonight are a few charred popcorn kernels and my bruised ego."

An older tenant from downstairs grumbles about how he's going to miss the end of his true crime show. A few ladies chime in, less than thrilled to be standing in the chilly night air. As much as I like Jake, I'm kind of on the neighbors' side with this one. I'm two inches of fabric away from mooning the entire apartment complex. At least it's dark.

Alice unzips the bright floral hoodie she's wearing, takes it off, and proceeds to tie it around my waist. "Take this, you beautiful goddess. While I process my jealousy over the fact that your legs are twice as long as mine, we can at least give you a little more privacy." As she knots the sleeves around me, she nods, satisfied with her handiwork.

"You're a lifesaver." I smile down at her. I love a girls' girl.

Alice pulls me away from the crowd to whisper conspiratorially. "Sleeping in Jordan's shirts now, huh? Careful. That's exactly how it started with me and Mr. Popcorn Scorcher over there."

She hooks a thumb in Jake's direction. Alice and I really do have a lot in common.

It's pointless trying to hide what's happening. Her boyfriend lives in the same apartment as the guy I'm seeing. They're bound to see and hear things. Plus, I'm standing in front of her half-naked. Besides, I'm dying to talk about it with someone.

"Actually, speaking of scorching, things got pretty hot with Jordan earlier," I admit.

"OH MY GOD! I KNEW IT!" When a dozen heads turn our way, she lowers her voice to a whisper. "Details. Now. Out with them."

"I don't know what to say. It just sort of happened." I shrug.

Alice beams. "Of course it did. Look at the two of you. You're both irresistible. It was bound to happen eventually. Frankly, I'm shocked it took this long."

"I can't deny Jordan is a fine specimen of a man. But it's more than that. He makes me feel…grounded?"

"Aw. I love this for you." She swoons.

I look over to where Jordan's standing on the curb, patiently nodding along as he listens to dozens of baseball questions and some unnecessary advice about the upcoming games from the older tenants who, as irritated as they are with our current situation, seem happy to have his undivided attention. I give him a small wave, and when he smiles at me, my nerves settle. He's keeping everyone calm, just by being here.

Being around him soothes something inside me, and I'm feeling fully myself for the first time in a long while. When I'm with Jordan, I'm not trying to look and sound smart, the way I act in school. I don't feel like I need to be on my best behavior, like I do at home.

I'm not tip-toeing around his feelings and being careful with my words so I don't set him off, the way I have in the past around my brother. For the most part, with Jordan I can just be me and know he can handle whatever that means. He's going to be traveling for a stretch of away games next week, and I feel like I already miss him. It's scary how attached I've already become. I know I shouldn't. I'll be leaving North Bay soon.

"Does Mike know about you two?" Alice asks.

"No," I respond too quickly. "Please don't say anything to Danielle either." I beg her with my eyes.

"I won't," she promises. "I get it. I really, *really* do. But can I give you some advice?" When I nod, she continues, "I've learned from experience that loving someone out loud feels so much better than trying to hide it. Even if your family doesn't agree with your choice, owning it is freeing."

"I don't know if I'm ready to chance it," I admit. "I know Jordan. He won't want to be the reason I fall out with my family. If Mike gets upset, Jordan will back away. And if that happens, I'll never be able to forgive my brother. Besides, I won't be in town long. I'm going back to D.C. soon."

She places a comforting hand on my arm. "It's a tough spot to be in." That's an understatement. "But he looks at you the same way you look at him. And if it comes down to any kind of a choice, I'd be willing to bet money that man will choose you."

I wish I were confident enough to agree with her. Unfortunately, I'm not.

It takes another twenty minutes until the fire department is finally able to sweep the building and give the all-clear. When the incessant beeping of the alarm finally stops, everyone breaks out in applause. Except Jake, whose hands are in the pockets of his jeans as he looks at the trees, still avoiding eye contact with Alice, who is glaring daggers at him.

At least most of the neighbors are too preoccupied with Jake's blunder to care about my bare lower half. Once we're allowed back into the building, I untie the sweatshirt and hand it back. Jake and Alice disappear into the guys' apartment holding hands, so I guess he's officially forgiven. I walk behind Jordan back into my place. Closing the door, I lean my head against it and let out a long sigh.

Just when I think this night can't get any more dramatic, my phone buzzes with another text from my brother.

Mikey: *Where were you earlier?*

Me: *Around. Everything's fine. You worry too much.*

Chapter 30

Jordan

My duffle bag is barely shoved in the door before I turn from my apartment and jog down the hall to Shelley's door. As soon as she opens it, I wrap my arms around her waist. She smells faintly of coffee from the part-time summer gig she picked up at Brew-Ha-Ha. She squeals when I lift her two inches in the air and spin her around before setting her feet on the ground and squeezing her in a tight hug. It's been four weeks since she moved in, and I love that she was waiting here for me to get home from our stretch of away games.

"Welcome home." Her words are muffled because her mouth is pressing into the collar of my shirt.

"Miss me?"

"Maybe." Shelley laughs. "I have a confession." She pulls away just enough to look into my face, which I'm sure is now laced with curiosity. I let go reluctantly, and I already miss her warmth. I raise a curious brow and wait for her to continue.

"I bought you food while you weren't here to argue. We're having chicken wings. A lot of them." She grabs a white paper bag dotted with spots of grease, then she points to a shipping box on the counter. "And I ordered four different kinds of sauce. I thought we could taste test them like that show. You know, see who can handle the heat. Are you hungry?"

I chuckle. "Are you going to make me answer really personal questions while I'm sweating out of my eyes, like they do?"

"Well, I wasn't. But you've gone and put the idea in my head, so now it has to happen."

"Obviously." I nod and head over to her cabinets to pull down two plates and glasses. "Water or milk? How hot are we talking?"

"Both. The answer is always both."

"A woman after my own heart."

I set the dishes down on the counter and go back to take the milk jug from the fridge. I hand a glass to Shelley and she smiles at me while I pour for her. Then she puts her drink on the breakfast bar and situates herself on a stool, dividing the wings between our plates. When she's satisfied that the plates are even, she moves on to opening each bottle of hot sauce and lining them up according to their Scoville scale ratings.

I love how seriously she's taking this. She looks at me and smirks while she arches an eyebrow. "Laugh it up now. My prediction is you'll be crying by wing three."

"Oh, probably sooner than that," I confirm. "I didn't grow up with a lot of exposure to spicy foods."

"Right. Whereas in rural Idaho I developed a well-rounded palate by sampling the world's most unique cuisine." She rolls her eyes. "We'll be fine. I only got mild, medium, and hot. Nothing super crazy."

"Okay, but if I puke up hot sauce while we're running sprints at practice tomorrow, I'm telling Coach it was your fault."

"I can live with that." Her bubbly excitement is contagious as I pull up the stool next to hers. She pours the first sauce onto a wing on my plate, then one of her own. "All right. One. Two. Three."

We each take a bite at the same time.

"Okay, I can handle this one. Can we stop now? Call it a success."

"You wish." She swivels her stool to face me, and when she giggles, I immediately know I would do anything to hear that sound again. I don't care how many Scovilles I need to consume.

She raises her eyebrows. "I was told you would be answering personal questions. We can take turns to keep it fair. Tit for tat and all."

"Tit for tat, huh?" My eyes start to travel down her body on their own accord. She tisks and wags a finger, so I have to pull my focus back to her face. "Hit me. What do you want to know now?"

Shelley taps her chin dramatically, which causes a little bit of sauce to rub off on her face.

"Oh, you have…" I reach out to take it off with my thumb, but she's starting to ask her question, so her mouth is open, and somehow my finger brushes her tongue. "Sorry. I was trying to do, uh…that." I quickly wipe the smudge of red sauce. Her eyes lock with mine, and she holds my wrist and brings my thumb back to her lips so she can suck it clean. I think my brain has short-circuited.

"Wouldn't want to waste it now, would we?" She turns and picks up her second wing, adding the next sauce like nothing happened.

Like I'm not sitting here realizing I'm falling in love with my best friend's little sister.

I clear my throat to remove the lump now lodged in it and say, "You were about to ask me something?"

"Oh, right. I was thinking. I still don't know much about your life before North Bay. Tell me everything. What was little Jordan like before he was a big, bad baseball player?"

"While I appreciate the sentiment, let's refrain from saying the words 'bad baseball player' in the same sentence as my name. That has to be bad luck."

"Ah, finally. The superstitious side everyone is always telling me about makes an appearance. Okay. Let's go with *big, strong baseball player*," she corrects herself. "Does that work for you?"

"Much better, thank you." I nod. "I'm from Baltimore. Just outside the city. It's not a terribly original story. Single mom. She tried, but my mom is not what I would call naturally maternal. She did what she could to support us, so she wasn't around a lot. My dad wasn't around either, but that was for a different reason. He was locked up when I was pretty young. He got out for a while, but then was in and out of prison for stuff like parole violations. Last I heard, he was in again." I take a sip of the milk before going on. "He was nice enough the few times I got to hang out with him. We would watch TV together if he was there. I remember he liked the Ninja Turtles. But I hardly know the guy, if I'm being honest." I sigh. Maybe I should feel more toward my old man, one way or another, but I don't. "My mom tried her best, but motherhood was more than she bargained for. Once I was old enough to be on my own, she seemed relieved to be rid of the burden."

Shelley listens to me intently, the hot sauce bottle in her hand suspended in mid-air.

"I remember when Danielle gave you that Ninja Turtle last year. I could tell it meant something to you, but I wasn't sure why. You could never be a burden, Jordan."

I shrug, not wanting to dwell on unpleasant memories. "That sounds like something the Carvers would say. My high school coach and his wife really stepped up for me."

"Can you tell me about them?" she asks, setting down the bottle.

"When I met Coach Carver, my mom and I were having a rough go of it. By then my dad was locked up for the long haul. My mom and I bounced around a lot between relatives and subsidized housing. Sometimes Coach would bring clothes to practice and tell me they were hand-me-downs his son had outgrown. He'd ask if I could do him a favor and take them off his hands. I think the Carvers bought them new for me, though, because everything was always in really good condition, and once or twice the tags were still attached. They had me over to their house for dinner a lot."

"Mrs. Carver is the one who taught you how to cook, right?"

"Yep. I call her Ms. Ruth. And that's pretty much my entire life story. Now you." I reach for the medium bottle and put a dab on my next wing.

"You already know my story. You've met all the key players. The truth is, when school is in session, I don't have much of a life outside of it."

"That makes sense. Law school must be hard."

"It's a lot of work," she admits.

"Understandable. But if we're really doing tit for tat here, you're going to need to give me more than 'law school is work.' I showed you my frayed edges. Now I get to see a little bit more of yours."

"You've already seen those, and yet you're still here," Shelley muses.

"Not all of them. I know you're still angry with your brother. Can you tell me more of that story? I've only heard it from him."

"Well, Mike's story is my story, too, in a way. Addiction affects the whole family. We had the whole white picket fence thing down pat, right up until we didn't. I got dragged along for the ride while my brother did his best to tear the Miller family apart."

It's hard to hear her talk about Mike this way. I didn't know him then, but I see how hard he works now, not only to better himself, but to help other people do the same. But I keep my thoughts to myself and only offer a sympathetic hum.

"I know it wasn't intentional," she assures me. "Addiction is a real disease. I shouldn't complain. My sisters and I always had what we needed." The way her face pinches tells me she feels guilty about this after what I just shared about my home life.

"It's okay to complain, Shelley. If it still hurts, it sounds like you didn't actually have what you needed."

She lets out a long, slow breath. "My job was to lay low and not cause any trouble. I ran track and got good grades. Tried to stay out of everyone's way. It wasn't hard because no one was paying attention anyway. When you have a sibling in crisis, all the resources are thrown that way, and you get whatever scraps of attention are left."

"So, you were taking care of yourself and your sisters?" I prompt. From what I know of the Millers, it's hard to imagine there was a time when their parents weren't doting on all their daughters.

"I mean, not totally," she says, taking another bite. "Mmm. I think this sauce might be my favorite. It's spicy but sweet, and you can actually taste the peach flavor." When I nod my agreement, she continues her story. "My parents are good people. They were just…preoccupied. There were a lot of times. I was the one making sure we all brushed our teeth or got up for school on time. I would sign Mandy and Maddy's homework folders or heat up canned ravioli for dinner. I was the only one of us old enough to drive, so I took them to their sports practices. I was the one doing our laundry."

"I get that. I feel similarly about my own mom. She wasn't a bad parent when she was around, she just wasn't around very much. And speaking of dinners heating up…" I hold up my next wing and touch it to hers in cheers. We each take a bite. As soon as the heat hits my throat, I start coughing. "That one's way more intense."

"Yeah, it is." Her eyes are wide as she agrees, reaching for her glass of milk.

When we've made our way through every sauce and washed our hands and faces clean, Shelley turns to me, offering a stick of gum, which I accept. After I take it from her, she touches her fingers to my chest and my entire body rumbles to life at the contact.

"Do you want to take this to the bedroom?" she asks.

After everything we shared tonight, there's an extra layer of weight to her question. We've done plenty of fooling around over the past few weeks, but I have yet to sink inside her. I know Shelley's still nervous about how her body will react to internal stimulation, but I think we're both craving the intimacy.

"I do," I assure her, putting my hands on her waist. "But only if you're ready." Her skin is warm under the fabric of her shirt.

I hear her sharp intake of breath. "This is real, isn't it?" she whispers. I can smell the hint of her cinnamon gum in the air passing between us.

"It's real," I confirm. I feel it too. The way I can sense her walk into a room before I see her because the air changes and my body responds. The way I look forward to her messages, and the pang of disappointment that hits hard if we miss even one day of saying goodnight.

"That scares me," she admits.

"It scares me a little, too. But in a good way."

My eyes drift down to her soft, full lips, then back to her eyes. There are tears starting to well and threatening to spill over, but she's smiling. A magnetic force pulls her even closer to me until her chest touches mine and there must be less than half an inch between my mouth and hers.

"Please kiss me," she whispers so softly that I'd think I imagined it if it weren't for the fact that we're standing so close I can feel the air as those words pass through her lips.

I tip my head forward to close the last little bit of distance between us. Her hands find their way up to my neck and pull me in while her lips part to grant me deeper access. She makes a sound somewhere between a hum and a moan, and it awakens the primal part of my brain that will do anything to keep her making those noises for me.

"I really want you, Jordan," Shelley admits.

"I know," I tell her, pulling her in for a hug and rubbing my hand on her back, trying to offer some comfort because I can anticipate where her thoughts are going next. I understand that she's still worried about her body. She's done such a good job talking about it. "I want you, too. Thank you for trusting me. And if nothing happens tonight, that's fine, too."

She backs away, wincing as she inhales a shallow, shaky breath.

"Did I say something wrong?" I only want her to know she can trust me not to push her. "Take a deep breath." I take a step toward her, but she takes another step back. I can see her mood shifting. Maybe talking about the past really got to her. "Shelley, talk to me. It's okay."

"It's not okay, though, Jordan. It's not. And I'm tired of pretending it is. All I want is to be normal and let these things happen the way they should. I don't want to need more deep breaths!" She groans and tugs at the hair at her scalp. "I'm sorry."

"Can you tell me what's the matter?" I thought I knew, but… "I'm kind of in the dark over here. I thought we were on the same page tonight?"

"We are," she says. "We just poured our hearts out to each other, and now we want to be intimate, like normal people should. But you're already expecting my body to fail tonight, and if I'm being honest, so am I. Failure is my default setting this year, and we both know it. I've tried so many appointments and medicines. You finally want to be physical with someone, and my body is still broken. Maybe not as much as it was in the beginning. But I don't want to fail at this with you."

"Whoa. Slow down. Can you explain what you mean?"

"You're so good at this. But I'm not. You're offering me everything I've been looking for, but so much is still against us, it's all because of me, and I can't do anything about it." Her arms raise as her volume increases. "My body is broken, and my mind won't shut up. And after all the appointments and medication, still the best advice anyone can offer is, 'Remember air exists?!' There is no amount of deep breathing that will fix it, and it's not fair." Her chest heaves as she finishes her speech.

"Hey." I close the gap she created between us and place my hands on her shoulders. "You're right about it not being fair. But we're in this together. You and me." I wave a hand between us. "And maybe I don't fully understand what it's like to be inside your body or your head. But I do know a thing or two about wishing I could get my body to do something it just won't. Believe me, I know how frustrating that is."

She shakes me off and steps away again. "It's not the same. Maybe you can't throw as hard or as far as you used to, but you can still throw better than most people in the country. This is different than your elbow injury. My reproductive system is going to affect every relationship for the rest of my life."

Her words sting as I let them sink in. I thought we were on the same page, but maybe we're not. The idea of her even considering other relationships makes me see red.

I shake my head. "No. It won't."

Shelley huffs and rolls her eyes. Then she crosses her arms while she fixes a hard stare on my face. "How exactly do you plan to stop it?"

I stalk toward her, cupping her face in my hands.

"Because I intend to be the only man who touches you from this point forward. I don't know if we'll ever get to feel you shatter underneath me again, and I can't make you any promises about that. But I can damn well promise I'm going to do whatever it takes to be the man you need, inside the bedroom and out of it. And I'll relish every second of our time together for as long as you let me."

A shiver runs through her. I can see it in the way her shoulders move and the tiny hairs on her arms stand at attention.

There it is.

I know she feels this pull as much as I do.

"Jordan," she whispers, finally surrendering.

I nod, encouraging her. "Ask for what you want, Sweetheart."

"I don't know if it will work, and I'm scared. But I do think I'd like to try."

"Sure. We can do that. Meet me at my place in twenty minutes?"

I prepared for this.

Chapter 31

Shelley

Exactly twenty minutes later when I knock on his door, Jordan wordlessly leads me to his room, where my breath catches in my throat.

It's perfect.

He thought of everything.

I can tell Jordan put so much effort into making this night special for me. He works so hard to give me what I need. He must have been planning this for a while, and I almost ruined it by getting stuck in my head. We have the place to ourselves. The sheets smell like detergent, the lighting is dim, and he has an entire playlist of the nature sounds and instrumental music I told him I prefer.

We sit together on the bed and his mouth trails kisses along my jawline, starting behind my ear and continuing until his lips find mine. He follows my lead and doesn't push for anything more than I want to give. When I think I'm ready, I slowly lower both of us onto the mattress and we start to peel away our clothes.

Jordan takes his time, caressing my arms, my legs, and my back. He dips his head to lavish attention on my breasts as he skates two fingers across my stomach.

I want to be here with him in this moment, but despite everything he's doing, my body's still not responding. I want it to. But it just…won't.

As much as I want him, I know if he goes any lower, he's going to feel how dry I am, and I don't want to insult him. Plus, my left hip keeps making popping and cracking noises every time I shift my position. Now I'm drowning in my thoughts again, frustrated with myself because about twenty percent of my attention is focused on my hip and the rest of me is fighting against my building anxiety. I don't have anything left to give to him, but I don't want to disappoint him or make him think I don't want this. I do.

"Shelley? What is it?" Jordan asks as though he can sense my spiraling thoughts. He's patient while he brushes my hair out of my face and tucks it behind my ear. With that small gesture, I suddenly notice how much my hair is sticking to my neck and driving me crazy. I wish I could put it up in a ponytail, but I can't do that if I'm going to be lying on my back like this because the bump from my hair tie will also be distracting.

"Nothing." I shift, trying to get comfortable and bring myself back to the moment with him, but I can't, which only frustrates me further. I can feel my eyes starting to burn, and I really do not want to melt down for a second time tonight in front of this man.

Jordan's been so kind. So patient. He deserves so much better than this. Better than me.

He sits up and puts his shirt back on.

"Are you mad?" I blink quickly, the burn in my eyes intensifying.

"No. Not at all," he reassures me, gently. "But I can see you're still uncomfortable. Can you tell me what's going on in there?" he asks, running his hand over my head. "Please?"

I sigh and resolve that it's best to be honest, so I launch into my explanation, spewing out every last thought that's been on my mind since we walked into the room. He sits still and listens.

"My joints keep popping, and I don't know what to do with my hair because if I put it back, then it pulls at my scalp, but if I leave it down, it gets in the way. I shaved this morning, but I can already feel stubble on my legs, which means I know you can feel it too, and that's annoying and distracting. You put so much effort into all of this." I gesture around the room. "I know I'm disappointing you, and that makes me so sick with myself, which makes it even worse. It's hard to feel sexy when you're irritated. I don't want those to be the thoughts in my head ruining what should be so special. You've done all of this for me." My eyes scan the space. "But those thoughts *are* here, and I hate it." I dig the heels of my hands into my eyes and tug on the roots of my hair. "I feel so stupid. You've seen me naked before. I don't know why I'm acting like this is such a big deal."

Jordan scoots a little closer. "Hey. First of all, I appreciate your concern about me, that's really sweet. But please don't assume how I'm feeling about something. I'm fine. And like I told you earlier, I'll continue to be fine if nothing happens tonight. I'd never want you to do something that made you feel this bad just to try to make me happy. As for the rest, it *is* a big deal to share yourself with someone. Every time. It doesn't matter what's happened in the past."

I understand where he's coming from, but that doesn't make it any easier.

"I know that. I feel the same way. At least theoretically. But everything has the potential to make me feel like this. Literally everything. I can't predict it, and it's not fair to ask you to be with someone who won't ever be able to fully meet your needs. I don't think I can do this."

Jordan deserves the world, not a loose cannon like me who blows a gasket whenever he tries to do or say something kind. Not to mention, I'm still too much of a coward to tell my family about him.

"Whoa. Hang on. What are you saying?"

"I can't do this to you, Jordan." I place my hand over his. "What you did here tonight is one of the kindest things anyone has ever done for me. No one has ever put in so much effort to make me feel seen. But I think I need to work on myself a little bit more before I'm in a place where I can commit to this level of a relationship with someone." It's already breaking my heart to know I'm making him suffer. "You're looking for something serious. You told me that from the beginning. But I'm only here for a few more weeks. Our time together is limited, and look how I'm wasting it. I can't do this to you. I won't. Not to mention we're still hiding from everyone. We still have all the same problems that made you say no to me in the first place, and here I am adding new ones. We shouldn't do this."

He turns away, and a piece of my soul shatters when his words turn cold. "So, I get no say here at all?"

"Jordan. You know I'm right."

He's silent for a long time before he swallows and nods. "If that's how you feel, you should go."

My heart cracks wide open, raw inside my chest, and I know it's true. I need to leave before I completely lose myself. I scramble to get dressed. After I tuck my phone into my pocket, I reach out to squeeze his hand once more, but he pulls away at the contact.

I force my legs to carry me out of his apartment. I turn toward my own door, but I can't be here right now. I need air.

Running down the steps, I burst through the front door of the building, letting it slam shut behind me. I make it three steps toward the parking lot before the first sob escapes my throat. I don't know how long I stand there, arms clutched around my stomach, giving in to the grief. We could have built something so good together. If only I weren't me.

How do you mourn something you never really had?

Sniffling, I reach into my pocket to see if I have a tissue, and realize not only do I not have one, but I also don't have my keys. My heart sinks even further. In my hurry to get to his place, I think I left them on my kitchen counter. Jordan would probably still let me sleep in his apartment, but there's no way I can go back up there and face him again tonight.

I can barely see through the tears as I dial my brother's number.

Chapter 32

Shelley

"Shelley?" Mike picks up on the second ring.

"Can you come get me?" I whimper, pathetic and broken.

"What happened? Where are you?"

"Outside the apartment. I locked myself out. Can I stay with you tonight? Please."

"Sure, but Jordan should be home tonight. He's right there. You can call him. I'm sure he'll help you get back in."

"No. I can't talk to him. I can't. Mikey, please," I beg.

His tone turns serious. "I'll be there in fifteen minutes."

And he is. My brother's truck is barely parked before he jumps out the driver's side. He takes one look at my tear-streaked face and I don't have to say another word. Mike isn't stupid. He knows.

"It was you? You were the one in the shower?" He runs a hand through his hair, his nostrils flaring while he seethes.

"Please don't do this right now."

"I'll kill him." He runs past me and bounds up the concrete steps behind me, heading straight for Jordan's third floor apartment.

"No, Mikey! Just take me home," I call up after him, but it's no use because he's already run ahead. I wipe my face and reluctantly follow him back up to the unit I just left. The door is open, and Jordan is sitting on the couch, looking as hurt and sad as I feel.

"Get up!" Mike barks at him. "What the hell is going on?" He points at me, demanding his friend answer for my tears. "What did you do?"

"He didn't do anything. It was me," I start, but my brother is too distracted by his own anger to listen.

A neighbor pokes her head out of her door to eavesdrop, so I step inside and close the door behind me to give us some privacy.

Mike's voice continues to rise, although I can tell he is fighting to keep calm, probably for my sake. "My sister?! Are you serious right now?"

Jordan is still sitting, but he turns to face Mike fully, resting his elbows on his knees, his folded hands hanging between his legs. He slowly lifts his chin. "I don't know what you want me to say, Miller. Shelley can speak for herself." His words are measured, but he sounds exhausted and defeated. I can relate.

I wipe my eyes again with the back of my hand and start to explain. "Look, Mikey, not that it's any of your business, but Jordan didn't do anything I didn't ask for."

That was the wrong thing to say. Jordan's face falls, and he quickly brings a hand up to cover his expression, but I can still see the pain in his eyes.

"You think you asked for it?!" My brother turns his head in my direction, fuming.

"That's not what I meant. I'd rather not get into details. Trust me, you don't want to hear them," I say.

Mike's eyes widen and his ears turn an unnatural shade of red as his head snaps back toward his friend.

Jordan groans from his place on the sofa, then brings himself to stand and square off. He's fighting to keep his voice steady. "I know what it sounds like. And what this looks like. I swear, I'd never hurt her. At first, I was just trying to help. Then it escalated. Things got out of hand tonight. I think we were both disappointed in the outcome."

The redness fades from Mike's features, but he's still seething as he stands still and quiet, trying to process.

"What do you mean *things got out of hand*?"

"She told you, you don't want to know."

"You know what? I think I do. And you better start talking. Now, Jordan."

"Mike—" I try to reason, but my brother cuts me off, still yelling at his friend.

"My sister just called me sobbing. Imagine my shock when I learned she needed me to come and pick her up because she locked herself out, but she couldn't stand the thought of being near my best friend." Jordan winces, but Mike doesn't stop. "I knew something was wrong. How long have you two been sneaking around like this?"

"Not long," Jordan says at the same time that I admit, "Since Idaho."

My brother spins toward me again, his face twisted with the hurt from our betrayal. "That was a month ago."

"Nothing serious happened until recently." I know in my soul it's a lie. We may not have gone all the way physically, but I gave Jordan my entire heart.

"Apparently, nothing is happening at all," Jordan corrects.

Hearing him dismiss our connection so casually tears the gaping hole in my chest further open, but I can't argue with him. I did this. To all of us.

Mike scrubs a hand down his face. "I swear to god, one of you better start making sense. I'm about five seconds away from completely losing my shit here."

I crack a weak smile. "I think it might alrcady be lost."

He points at me. "Not. Funny."

It's not, and my reaction is completely inappropriate for the situation. I almost feel sorry for Mike, but it's been an emotional night, and one sad smile turns into a reluctant laugh, which causes Jordan to relent with a smile and a small chuckle of his own.

My poor brother is so confused and frustrated with us that he throws both hands in the air. He looks to Jordan first. "Explain."

"A couple months ago, Shelley meant to send a voice memo to someone else, but she accidentally sent it to me instead."

Mike's brows pinch together and his mouth twists into a confused expression. I'm quick to add, "You really don't need to worry about it."

"The fact that you called me here in the middle of the night and you've both been so secretive about this says otherwise," my brother deadpans.

"We were trying to avoid this exact reaction," I rationalize, but I know it's not entirely fair. This is a lot to throw at Mike at once. It's not like we gave him a chance to react any differently. Still. "Fine. You want the truth?"

"Yes!" He huffs, frustrated and impatient.

"Okay, but you asked for this," I warn. "I didn't think you'd want to hear I was having trouble achieving orgasm, and thought I needed some assistance."

My brother's eyes widen and his nostrils flare again.

Jordan winces and takes a step back, probably afraid that Mikey's going to take a swing at him. "I wouldn't phrase it exactly like that." He raises both hands in front of him, placating my brother.

"How *would* you phrase it?" Mikey crosses his arms, staring him down.

Jordan takes a breath, and there's a long pause as he considers the question. "Okay, I guess I would phrase it like that," he admits. "But I really was just trying to help her, man."

"Sisters. Are. Off. Limits!" My brother bellows.

Jordan nods. "I know. I told her the same thing at the beginning. We never meant for it to get this far."

I'm truly starting to get annoyed with them for talking about me like I'm not here, or worse, like I belong to Mike and can't make my own decisions about who I let into my life. "I'm not some baseball card you can order your friends not to touch!" I snap at my brother. "I decide who I can and can't talk to."

The veins in Mike's neck pop and he clenches his teeth before grinding out, "I know. You're way more valuable than that, Shell. And, again, *you're t*he one who called *me* over here to help, remember?"

I guess I should be glad we're glossing over the whole lack-of-orgasm admission, but this is getting ridiculous.

"Look, Jordan was amazing tonight. He was kind, and thoughtful, and sweet. He was a perfect gentleman." My voice is rough because I've sobbed my throat raw. I chance a look at Jordan and immediately wish I hadn't, because the searing pain pierces my chest yet again when my eyes lock with his. "I just couldn't bring myself to do anything physical tonight. So he stopped—exactly like he should have—and I left. I knew I'd never be able to give him what he needed with this brain and this body." My voice cracks on the final word, and I stop talking because the sobs are threatening to choke me again.

"Shelley," Jordan whispers. He starts to take a step in my direction, but he freezes when I shake my head.

I wipe another stray tear away with the palm of my hand and turn to my brother. "Can we please go now? I'll call a locksmith in the morning."

"Yeah. Fine." Mike tosses me his keys and motions to the door. "Wait in the truck. I'll be down in a minute. I'm not finished with him."

I want to protest, but I don't have any fight left in me. So I leave, forcing myself not to look back.

Chapter 33

Jordan

Miller paces in front of me while he rubs his jaw with one hand. He shakes his head, still seeming at a loss for words until he finally barks at me. "Talk."

"I'm really not sure you want to hear this."

How am I supposed to give him details about why Shelley came to me asking for advice? He might think he wants to know, but I can promise he doesn't.

"Oh, I definitely do. What the hell, Jordan? Start explaining."

"It started a few weeks before your wedding. Like we told you, she accidentally sent me a message meant for someone else, and then we started talking sort of regularly. She needed advice, and I was trying to be a good friend."

"A good friend would direct her to her brother for advice."

"I don't think either of you would've been comfortable with that."

"What can my sister say to you that she can't say to me?"

He looks so hurt and defeated, but it really wasn't the betrayal he thinks it is. I take a deep breath and shake my head. "She just had a lot of questions, and she wanted to talk to a guy she could trust to be real with her but not get creepy. Those are her words. We weren't trying to keep you in the dark about anything back then. Well, I guess we sort of were. But not in a nefarious way. Just in a 'this would be awkward to say to your brother' way."

"So, to be clear, you've been sneaking around with my little sister for months and giving her sex lessons?"

"Don't make it sound underhanded. It wasn't like that."

"Wasn't it, though? Why else would you feel the need to hide that you were talking to her?"

"You don't understand."

"No, *you* don't understand because you don't have anyone in your life who means as much to you as my sisters mean to me." His words land with a thud in my gut, and I swallow the little bit of bile that rises in my throat. I can't even argue. It's true. I don't have any family who would step in for me the way the Millers are there for each other. And after this, I might not have them either. When he sees the stricken look on my face, Mike tries to walk it back. "Shit. That's not what I meant."

"Yes, it is. And maybe you're right. We knew it would be hard for you to hear. Look, I'm sorry you found out this way. I am. But I'm not sorry for trying to be her friend. Shelley didn't want to talk to you about it. The same way you don't run to her when you need to talk to someone about a craving. Not every topic is sibling-safe."

Mike sighs and pinches the bridge of his nose. It might not be fair for me to use his addiction that way, but the gloves are off now. I want him to see he's being a hypocrite here. He doesn't get a say in

Shelley's love life, and he has no business getting on her case for asking a few innocent questions. Or mine for trying to answer them.

"Be honest. Have you slept with her?" He looks straight at me. I don't answer, just hold his stare with one of my own. I told Shelley I wouldn't talk to him about this, and I'm not starting now. He heaves a disappointed sigh at my silence. "Just…keep your hands to yourself," he mutters.

"This isn't just about sex," I argue. "Mike, you know me. Isn't it better for her to be with your best friend than a total stranger?"

He hesitates. "…I really don't know."

I clamp my mouth shut because his attitude is starting to piss me off, and it's only confirming that Shelley was right when she said she couldn't talk to him.

Inhaling a long breath, I steel myself to say what I know I need to tell him. "Look, man. I'll always be ride or die for you. But you're way off base right now. I didn't fall for your sister on purpose, but it happened. I fell for her. Hard. I know she got scared tonight, and frankly, a lot of that is on you because we both knew you'd react this way. But I'm not going anywhere." I cross my arms and stare him down. "I know you can relate, even if you don't want to admit it. Can you honestly tell me you'd have walked away from Danielle if Honey disapproved?"

Danielle and her grandma are super close. Honey loved Mike from the beginning, but something tells me even if that hadn't been the case, it wouldn't matter. Other people don't get to dictate who we end up with.

His shoulders relax and he backs up a bit, but he doesn't answer, so I keep going. "Because I don't think that's how it would've gone down. I think you would've stuck it out and fought for each other. Even if it meant disappointing the people you care about. When you love someone, it's worth it."

There's a long pause before he asks, "You love Shelley?"

I don't hesitate for a second. "I do."

His eyes scan my face, looking for any sign I might be bluffing. He won't find it. He lets out a long, slow breath and moves over to the couch, taking a seat so he can think. It takes a minute, but eventually he says, "I think I believe you."

"Good, because it's the truth."

It's a long time before he speaks again. "You're right about one thing. If this is real, it doesn't matter what I think."

"That's what she said from the beginning. Unfortunately, I don't think she ever really believed it. She cares about your opinion. And so do I. Too much, if you want to know the truth."

Mike sighs. "I want my sister to be happy." After a beat, he adds, "And you, too, man. Or at least I will, eventually. It's just going to take me a little while to get used to the idea that you two could find that kind of happiness with each other. I can't say I like it. But I won't get in your way."

"Fair. We can try to stay out of your face."

"Nah. I don't want you to feel like you need to hide from me. That's what started all of this. It sucks that neither of you thought you could tell me. Falling in love should be a good thing."

Now he thinks my being with Shelley is a good thing? Bro is giving me whiplash, but I'm not going to question his sudden change of heart when I agree with him.

"We both hated going behind your back."

"I'm sorry. I guess I still have more shit to work through than I thought. I know you'll treat her right."

"I would hope it goes without saying, but I will. If she lets me. It's going to take a lot more convincing on that front. You weren't our only problem. But we're cool?"

He shakes his head, but stands to take my hand and pull me into a one-armed hug.

"I still really want to punch you," he admits while squeezing me.

"Yeah, well, same." I pat his back twice before we let go.

He can be mad, but I refuse to let this break us. Mike has become a brother to me, too. But sometimes brothers need to have it out. That's just the way it is. I know he only wants to protect Shelley. But he's not the only one worrying about her now.

Mike steps back and tucks his hands in his pockets. His shoulders rise while he says, "I hate seeing her like this. I've never seen her this frazzled. This isn't like her. How do we fix it?"

I shake my head. "I don't know if we can. But right now my plan is to keep showing up." Because the Millers are family to me, and that's what families should do.

Chapter 34

Shelley

The sound of the driver's side door opening pulls me from my swirling thoughts. Mike takes his seat in the parked truck and drums his fingers on the steering wheel, trying carefully to plan his words. Finally, he looks at me and asks the question I've been expecting. All my brother's confusion, anger, hurt, and disappointment are contained in one word.

"Why?"

He doesn't need to elaborate. I know the weight the word holds because I've asked myself the same thing for months. Why wouldn't I go to him? Why would I betray the trust he worked so hard to earn? Why would I secretly hook up with his best friend behind his back? Why did I lie, or at least omit where I've been lately, and let him worry? Above all, why am I so drawn to Jordan?

"I don't know." I look down at my hands as I fidget with them in my lap.

"Yes, you do," he protests. "Just talk to me, Shell. Please." I can hear a hint of insecurity poking through his tough exterior.

Blinking quickly, I raise my head and tip it back until I'm staring at the peeling fabric on the ceiling of his old pickup. "I never wanted to have this conversation. It hurts," I admit.

"Well, too bad. Avoiding it seems to be what got us here. You obviously have some things you need to say to me. So, let's do this."

I don't want to, but he's right. We need this.

"Mikey, I love you. But I need you to back off. I'm an adult, and I can make my own choices."

My brother shrugs. "So make them. I admit I'm not thrilled you were sneaking around, and maybe I could have handled things differently up there." He points to Jordan's window. "But ultimately, it's your decision. All I've ever wanted is for you to make good choices. And it's only because I don't want you to have to learn about life the hard way."

I groan. "Don't you see? I *did* learn about life the hard way. Mostly because of you. Going to Jordan *was* a good decision. He's done more for me over the past few months than anyone has in a long time." I sniffle. As much as I've tried to avoid this confrontation with my brother, it's been a long time coming. Avoiding this rift between us hasn't caused any of my resentment to go away.

Mike's words are cautious. "I'm trying to understand. If you're both so happy together, why are you sitting here looking miserable? He looked the same way. Go back upstairs and be with him."

"You think I don't want to do that?" I turn to him, my volume higher than I intended. "Of course, I'd rather be up there than sitting here suffering through this conversation. This is exactly why I've been dreading having this talk with you. It's not that simple, though, is it? Because I'm me, and you're you."

Mike's taken aback. "Me? What do I have to do with it?"

"Of course, you! I spend my entire life tiptoeing around your reactions. Why would this be any different?" I toss up my hands. "When you were using, I couldn't do anything that would set you off or pull focus away from you, because god forbid Mom and Dad had to spend a second of their time away from all your bullshit. Then you were clean, but nothing changed for me because I still couldn't cause any drama. Everyone was worried we might set you off and cause a relapse. So, I got good grades. And I handled our sisters. And I made my own way. I even applied to East Coast schools and moved across the country so *you* would still have family close by."

I suck in another shaky breath while the truth I've been holding finally tumbles out of me. "I did everything for everyone else, even when it pushed me to the breaking point. And not one person noticed or cared. Not until Jordan."

"Shelley," Mike says softly, but I ignore him and continue to spill the truth I've been holding for too long.

"But Jordan was *your* friend before he was mine. He cares about you, and he wanted to put *you* first, just like everyone always does." It wasn't a surprise. Jordan is loyal, steady, and supportive. It's just who he is. Of course he would prioritize his best friend. "Did he tell you he didn't even want to talk to me at first because he was worried about how you'd react? We both were. Deep down, I knew I couldn't ever really be with him. You need him more than I do. Plus, he deserves better than me anyway. I'm a mess, obviously," I confess, motioning to my tear-stained face.

"Shelley," my brother repeats my name, more assertively. "My issues aren't your responsibility. They never have been."

I huff out a sarcastic breath. "Right. Sure."

"They aren't. Look, I'm sorry that weight was forced on you. You have no idea how much I wish I could turn back the clock and do it all differently. But I can't. What I *can* do is be your big brother now."

A groan of frustration escapes. "You still don't get it. That's exactly the problem! I wish you weren't involved in this at all. When are you going to stop treating me like a child and have at least a little bit of respect for my autonomy? I'm a whole-ass adult now."

Mike pinches the bridge of his nose. "Shelley, I wouldn't be here if I didn't respect you. You *asked* me to come. You called *me*, remember?"

I deflate, having no argument for that. "I know."

Here I am screaming at my brother, but I'm the one who pulled him into this. I'm the one who locked myself out of my apartment. Here we are again, with the truth slapping me in the face. My biggest problem is me.

I need a minute to collect myself before I say, "I'm sorry. I love you. I hope you know that. I'm just…having a hard time right now."

"I love you, too. I want to be here for you when things get like this," he says.

"I know. I'll try to work on being more open to it."

"Thank you. I'll try to work on backing off a little. But you're not alone, Shell."

I take a shaky breath. "Okay."

Mike shifts and pulls his phone out of his pocket, glancing at a text.

"I don't know if you want to hear this right now, but Jordan got the building manager to unlock your apartment. You can go back inside if you want."

The weight of the day threatens to pull me under. Tilting my head further back against the headrest, I squeeze my eyes shut. "No. Please just drive."

Mike nods and shifts the truck into gear. As he pulls out of the parking lot, my eyes are glued to the apartment in the rearview mirror.

Chapter 35

Jordan

"Here goes nothing," I mutter to myself, knocking on the front door of the small brick rancher. This has to work. When it opens, Mike slips outside to greet me. "Is she still here?" I ask, cautious but hopeful. It's been two days since I've seen Shelley at the apartment. I have to believe this plan might win her back. I know she's going back to school soon, and I'll never forgive myself if I don't try.

He nods. "Yeah. You sure about this?"

"I've never been more sure about anything."

Mike places a hand on my shoulder. "Just be good to her, man. She's not as tough as she wants you to believe." I guess this means he's gotten over his desire to punch me.

I tap his arm twice before I head inside. Shelley's sitting at the dining room table, talking to Danielle. When she notices me, her lips part and her eyes widen. Danielle turns to see what's causing the reaction.

"Jordan?"

"Shelley, can we talk?" I take a step toward her. She stands and rubs her palms on her jeans, looking as nervous as I feel.

"Um, okay." She leads me to the sofa and perches herself on the edge of the cushion next to mine.

"I know the other night didn't go the way either of us expected," I start. "And I've been thinking."

She eyes me curiously, waiting for me to go on.

So, I tell her, "First, I need to say I'm sorry."

Her brow creases. "You have nothing to apologize for. I'm the one who—"

"Yes, I do. I made you feel like the connection between us was something shameful, like it needed to be hidden. I dimmed your light, right from our first conversation. And you don't deserve that. You were made to shine." That must be the cheesiest thing I've ever said. But it's true, so I'm going with it. "I also want you to know I heard you, and all your concerns are valid. The distance is an issue, and school takes up a lot of your time. I know you're still concerned about your body. But I'm deep in this with you, Shelley. You carved your way in here." I say, laying a hand over my chest. "I can live without the physical stuff. We'll figure that part out together. I want to be with you. And I want everyone to know it."

She sighs. "I want that too. But I still don't know how it could work. We don't make sense, Jordan."

"That's why I'm here. To ask you a favor. Will you do something for me?"

Her eyes meet mine, questioning.

"Will you give me today? Just one day. Let me show you."

"Show me what?" There's a breathy thread of hope laced through her words.

"My closing argument. The way I should have handled this from the beginning. Let me show you how this could be. If we let it."

I stand and reach out for her. For a long moment Shelley sits, staring at my open palm. But then she slides her hand into mine, and I know. This is how it feels to be home.

"Where are we going?" she asks.

"You'll see." I squeeze her hand and lead her out to the car.

As we pull up to the park next to the library, I pop the trunk and retrieve the small cooler and patchwork quilt I packed. Then I guide Shelley to the gazebo. After spreading the blanket on the floor, I start unloading the contents of the cooler.

"I thought we could start with a light dinner. I brought turkey wraps." I take a candle and a lighter out of the cooler and flick on a flame, lighting the wick.

It's only ten-thirty in the morning, but she goes along with my plan and takes a seat for our picnic, her legs tucked under her. I hand her a sandwich and a small plastic bag filled with pretzels, followed by a bunch of grapes.

"This is nice," she says, glancing out at the expansive green park beyond our perch in the gazebo. There's a cool breeze blowing through the wooden slats. In the distance, we can hear the flowing water of the Chesapeake, and the occasional squawk of a bird looking for its breakfast. Otherwise, North Bay is quiet. We sit, taking small bites, both of us unsure of what to do or say. Finally, Shelley is the first to start.

"I'm so sorry."

I shake my head at her. "I'm not angry about the other night. You were only being honest. You should be able to tell me how you're feeling. I want you to. I just wish you hadn't run from it."

"Me too. I was scared," she admits, her eyes lowered to her half-eaten turkey wrap.

"Of me?" My stomach clenches at the thought. Did I push too hard? Did I make her feel pressured?

"Of this." Her crystal eyes meet mine, and she waves a hand in the space between us. "Of my feelings for you. They're intense, Jordan. I've never felt this way before. And I understand you might not fully feel the same way about me. And even if you do, my body won't always cooperate. I don't want to be a burden on you. Plus, the timing isn't exactly convenient, and I don't know how to handle any of it."

"Okay, well, first of all, I can confirm I have, in fact, caught feelings. *Intense* feelings. So many feelings." When I put my hand on her knee, she blushes. "I know we didn't get an ideal start. But if you're open to a do-over, so am I."

Shelley nods. "I'm very open to a do-over."

"Great. Let's finish our picnic, then we have another stop to make."

"Oh?"

"Remember the place where we went go-karting last year? They also have a retro-style arcade on-site. I have a jar of quarters in the car. I thought we could check it out."

She gasps as she figures out my plan. "This is the fantasy date, isn't it? The one I wrote about in my email."

I offer a small smirk and a wink. "I have no idea what you're talking about."

She hurries to finish the rest of her wrap in two bites. "Let's go! I'm ready!"

Chuckling, I tell her, "We don't need to rush anything. We can take all the time we need."

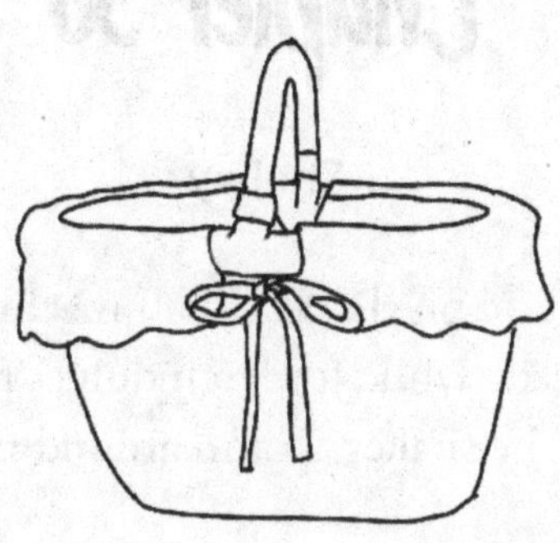

Chapter 36

Shelley

The lights and music on the Skee-Ball machine announce my win to the whole arcade while Jordan indulges my victory dance. As I moonwalk past him, he snakes an arm around my waist and pulls me in.

"Okay, Champ. Winner picks the next game. What do you want to do now?"

I scan the room until I spy a familiar game. "Pac-Man?"

"You're on." He keeps hold of me as we head across the floor. It's freeing to be out in public with him like this, with his arm around me, not worrying who might see.

When Jordan takes his turn at the machine, it becomes clear that I severely underestimated his Pac-Man skills, and he's kicking my butt this time. We're down to our last handful of quarters, and, as fun as this is, I'm looking forward to Phase Three of this date even more. I remember what I wrote, and the anticipation is killing me.

"I'm ready to head out whenever you are."

As soon as we get back to the car, Jordan reaches into the back seat and hands me a green box tied with a simple white ribbon.

"What's this?"

"A gift. I thought Mr. Fluffers needed someone to keep him company. You may be going back to school soon, but I don't ever plan on saying goodbye. So, this is just…" He motions for me to open it, and I untie the bow and lift the lid. Inside the box, a crocheted alligator is nestled in a bed of shredded newspaper. It's wearing a tiny t-shirt that says *See you later, Litigator.*

I bark out a laugh. "That might be the worst lawyer joke I've ever heard, but I love it. Did you make this?"

He nods. "The alligator, yes. I made it on the road when we had the game in Charlotte. I recalled somebody implying I should expand my crochet repertoire. The joke I can't take credit for. I bought the shirt pre-made from a website."

I didn't know it was possible for him to melt me any more than he already has, but he just keeps doing things like this. "Thank you. I love him. He needs a name."

"It's going to be hard to top Mr. Fluffers," Jordan teases as he starts to drive.

"Should we give him an A name since he's an alligator? Does he look like an Alvin to you? Or maybe an Alex? Something else? L for litigator? Lonny? Leonardo?"

"Leonardo the alligator?"

I shrug. "I think I like it."

"Then Leo it is."

I thought we were headed back to the apartments, but instead we drive out a bit further until we pull into the Marnock Hotel. He reserved Room 206, the same room from the night of the wedding. Jordan walks me to the door. He steps forward and puts his hands on my hips, gently tugging me toward him until our bodies touch. I'm still holding my alligator.

"I'll snuggle with him every night we're apart," I promise.

Jordan's smile comes back out to play. "This guy and Mr. Fluffers both get to share your bed while I'm not there? Are you trying to make me jealous?" His thumb hooks into my belt loop.

"Maybe a little."

One of his hands moves up to cup the back of my head while the other wraps around to the small of my back. I tilt my chin up to look into his eyes again, and his face hovers just above mine. "I know being apart will be hard when you go back to school. I'm not going to pretend it won't. But I believe in us. It will go so fast. You'll be busy while I finish out the season. Then we'll figure out what comes next. People have done much harder things than love someone who lived a few hours away. I'm not going anywhere. I love you, Shelley. Tell me you feel this, too."

One tear trickles down my cheek as I stare up at him. How did I get this lucky?

"Yes," I whisper. "Of course I feel it. I love you, too."

He brings his lips to mine, and I run my fingers through his hair while I pour everything I thought I would never be able to say to him into this kiss.

"Jordan?"

He hums a questioning noise into my mouth. I've never been more confident in anything than I am when I tell him exactly what I want.

"I think it's time for me to cash in that raincheck. Will you take me to bed?"

And he does. But not before I ask if he remembered to pack his jersey. There's still one more dream we can make come true.

Epilogue

Eight Years Later

Shelley

"**D**addy, can you fix my braids?" Janie runs into the living room with a crocheted bunny rabbit in one hand and a coloring book in the other. Jordan picks her up and spins her around, blowing raspberries into our four-year-old's belly until she dissolves into a fit of giggles. Then he takes a seat on the couch and sets her on his lap, expertly redoing the pigtails that have come undone from her roughhousing.

As he secures the second elastic, my husband kisses the top of our daughter's head and says, "Should we stick some waffles in the toaster for breakfast?"

"Can we put sprinkles and whipped cream on them?" Janie's eyes widen in delight.

Jordan smiles and nods. "And we'll fill all the squares with blueberries."

"Chocolate chips," Janie counters. She's a tough negotiator, like her mom.

As she scrambles off his lap, Jordan stands and I make my way over to wrap my arms around him. "I hate to say I told you so, but do you think after all these years you can finally admit toasters are a must-have?"

He looks down at me through his glasses as his arms circle my waist. "Oh, I think you love telling me that. But I concede. This time you were right, Counselor. How do you feel about the brief?"

I was up late last night working on a new case, and I need to head out soon if I'm going to beat the traffic on the way to the courthouse. It's a long commute from North Bay into Fredericksburg, but totally worth such a small sacrifice for our children to grow up surrounded by family.

Sighing, I shrug. "It's as good as it's going to get. I really do need to get moving. Have a great day with Janie."

"Always do." He smiles. "Will we see you for dinner?"

"I hope so, but it might be a late one for me. Don't wait if she's hungry."

He smirks and kisses my neck, his beard tickling my skin. "I'll feed her, but I don't mind waiting for *my* dinner." The mischievous tone in his voice hints that he's not talking about food at all.

I swat him away, playfully. "Maybe. We'll see how I'm feeling."

He puts a hand over the small bump in my belly and runs his thumb over the fabric of my blazer. We haven't shared our latest news with anyone else yet, and I love having a fun secret between us again. It reminds me of how everything started.

Jordan likes to joke that I once offered him my first-born child in exchange for helping me move, and he decided to take me up on it.

He still works part-time for Davis's company, doing inventory and serving as an extra set of hands if someone on the regular crew calls out sick. But for the most part, he's right here with us, which is exactly how we like it. Jordan's told me a thousand times he will never take our family for granted, and he wants to be the kind of dad he always wished he had. So far, I'd have to say he's knocking it out of the park. He loves being a stay-at-home dad, and Janie is equally obsessed with him. I love that I know she's in the best, most capable hands while I'm in the office.

And even when Jordan can't be here, someone always can. Our house is only a mile away from Mike and Danielle's place, and Janie is constantly over there playing with her cousins. Honey watches their three kids regularly, and she also helps take care of Janie on the days Jordan is working. She charges us an arm and a leg because, in her words, "all this life experience doesn't come cheap," and our toddler has picked up a few colorful phrases during their time together, but we all love it. My parents have also decided to retire, and they're looking into buying a vacation home in North Bay so they can split their time between here and Idaho. It will be nice to be close to them again.

Jordan kisses my nose. "Don't forget the Carvers are coming over tomorrow for the barbecue."

When he retired from baseball, Jordan was worried he wouldn't see the Carvers much, but that turned out to be an unfounded fear. Once he was no longer constantly traveling for work, he had a lot more free time available to schedule visits. He actually sees them much more often than he did when he was playing. They're another set of honorary grandparents for Janie.

"It's in my calendar. Do you need me to stop and pick up more hot dog buns?"

"Nah. We're going with chicken wings." He winks at me. Wings have been my biggest pregnancy craving, and at this point I could give Stacy Haverson a real run for her money.

"Yay! Grandma and Grandpa Carver!" Janie squeals. "Can I show them my new paint set? The one Uncle Jake and Aunt Alice gave me?"

Jordan's eyes soften as he turns to her. "I'm sure they'd love to see it. Now let's go get you those waffles. With chocolate chips *and* blueberries."

Thank you for reading!

If you enjoyed this book, please leave a review on sites like Amazon or Goodreads! Your reviews are so important to help independent authors spread the word about our books.

You can leave your review here.

Please join my newsletter at http://stephaniegiese.com to access bonus content from this series and find out the latest news about upcoming books and appearances.

Acknowledgements

It takes an entire team to make a book happen, and I am eternally grateful for every member of mine. First, to my family: my husband, Eddie, and our children: Nicholas, Abigail, Donny, Ana, and Penelope. Thank you for your constant support and encouragement as well as the gift of time. I know it's a huge sacrifice to give up so much time with your wife and your mom so that I can spend hours alone writing love stories about my imaginary friends. But you understand that this is the work that feeds my soul, and I will always appreciate the way you truly *see* me.

To my mother, Teri Wilkins, for reading every single one of my books and always giving them five stars, even when you're mortified by their content. I'm sure this one was no exception.

To my aunt and uncle, Charlotte and Sonny Hayman, for inviting me into your Virginia home every summer of my childhood and inspiring the town of North Bay.

To my sister, Charlotte Beckmeyer, who inspired much of Shelley's strong, independent personality and the banter between all the Miller sisters.

To my editor, Denise Drapeau, thank you for your patience and the care you took with this entire series to bring out the best in my characters and their stories.

My cover designer, Rachel Adams-Howard, for giving me adorable, cohesive covers and sticker designs that brought these characters to life.

Meredith Spidel and Ellen Williams, for your professional opinions regarding the mental health and medical references in this book.

My proofreader, Tara May, for catching as many errant commas and typos as possible before I send my words out into the world.

My bookish bestie, Kandice Coppala, for alpha reading early versions of this story before it really made sense and spending hours talking through Shelley and Jordan's personalities and character development.

My fabulous ARC and street team members, thank you for all your support for my books. I literally could not do this job without you. Your reviews, shares, and social media posts are the reason my books find new readers and I get to continue doing the best job in the world: dreaming up new ways for people to fall in love.

And finally, to all the readers. I appreciate you more than you will ever know. Thank you for spending your time in North Bay with me!

About the Author

Stephanie Giese lives in an overflowing house in Florida with her large family and one very naughty beagle. Stephanie likes to say she specializes in creating cozy chaos. She writes stories with humor and heart that have a strong focus on mental health, treatment, and consent. She is the author of the memoir *All I Never Knowed* as well as the North Bay romantic comedy series, which includes *Out of Left Field*, *Right as Rain*, and *Way Off Base*.

Other Books by Stephanie Giese

*If you loved **Way Off Base**, you might also like….*

<u>*Out of Left Field*</u> (2025) is Book One in the North Bay series. This small-town baseball romance is the story of minor league baseball player Mike Miller and his unexpected connection with Danielle Daniels, a local woman with deep roots in North Bay's crabbing community. Sometimes the best things in life pop up out of nowhere, but will these two be able to overcome their difficult pasts in order to let love in? Expect dad jokes, karaoke, and an adorable meet-cute over steamed crabs.

Right as Rain (2025) is Book Two in the North Bay series. Jake Gibson and Alice Caulfield grew up the best of friends until something tore them apart. Now all grown up and helping their mutual friend plan her wedding, a trip to retrieve some cupcakes leaves these frenemies stranded together in the middle of a hurricane in a tiny cottage with only one bed. As they learn to work together to overcome life's storms, lightning just might strike when they least expect it. Expect prank wars, a very lazy bulldog, and some creative uses of frosting.

A Crabby Little Christmas (2025) is a collection of holiday-themed short stories that are bonus material for the North Bay series. This fun quick-read features a story for each couple in the North Bay books as well as a bonus chapter from Grandma Honey. Expect ice skating, hot chocolate, and cozy Christmas vibes.

<u>*All I Never Knowed*</u> (2021) is a memoir written in collaboration with Stephanie's oldest son, Nicholas, who is now an adult. Written at his request, this is the true story of the Giese family and their fight through the American mental healthcare system for over a decade, desperately seeking resources for their oldest son as he struggles through childhood with severe mental illness. Expect to learn about a broken system while you laugh, cry, and get extremely frustrated on behalf of suffering children. The book also offers practical resources and support. The Gieses now use their story to help train first responders in how to respond to families in crisis with empathy and effective communication.